Everything You Need to Know About the Count of Monte Cristo

By Charles River Editors

19th century illustration of Edmond Dantès

About Charles River Editors

Charles River Editors was founded by Harvard and MIT alumni to provide superior editing and original writing services, with the expertise to create digital content for publishers across a vast range of subject matter. In addition to providing original digital content for third party publishers, Charles River Editors republishes civilization's greatest literary works, bringing them to a new generation via ebooks.

Introduction

Alexandre Dumas

The Count of Monte Cristo

"I have once again found a man ready to hack at another's self-respect with a hatchet, but who cries out when his own is pricked with a pin." – Alexandre Dumas, *The Count of Monte Cristo*

Playwright, novelist, travel writer, journalist, entrepreneur – it is hard to place Alexandre Dumas in one category alone, as his genres almost always influence one another. But most scholars and critics agree that he is clearly one of the greatest adventure novelists of all time. Responsible for such well-known titles *The Count of Monte Cristo, The Corsican Brothers, The Man in the Iron Mask*, and perhaps one of the most iconic and recognizable novels ever written, *The Three Musketeers,* the name Dumas has become synonymous with stories of drama, adventure, travel and intrigue featuring exceptional characters, exotic locales and fascinating journeys, both literal and figurative. His works have engaged readers all over the world, and been printed in over 100 languages.

The Count of Monte Cristo is now a staple of Western classrooms and has been made into many movies. The epic tale takes place in France, Italy, the Mediterranean Islands and the Levant from 1815-1838, spanning a generation of characters and growth. The book's protagonist, Edmund Dantès, is one of the most famous characters in literature, and the story follows him as he runs the gamut of emotions. Even today, the story's themes of hope, justice, vengeance and mercy fascinate readers of all ages.

The Count of Monte Cristo is entertaining for adults but also accessible for children, which is why so many schools assign it as reading. Of course, the novel is as lengthy as it is great, so it's hard to remember all the important stuff. *Everything You Need to Know About the Count of Monte Cristo* is a comprehensive guide that provides a synopsis, a description of the characters, and a summary and analysis of every chapter. You can use this as a guide while you read or as a way to brush up on everything you once knew and since forgot.

About Alexandre Dumas

Dumas was born Davy de la Pailleterie on July 24, 1802 in France to Thomas-Alexandre Dumas a highly decorated general in Napoleon's army. His father was also the first black general in the French army, and to this day holds the distinction of being the highest ranking European military official of color in history. Dumas's mother, Marie-Cessette Dumas, was an Afro-Caribbean slave. Although his father died when he was only four, leaving his mother and sister poverty-stricken, Marie-Cessette regaled her children with stories of their father's heroism and adventures, sparking young Alexandre's fascination with travel and historical adventure stories. In spite of their financial straits, the family was considered aristocracy due to Thomas-Alexandre's rank. As a result, they were well-connected, allowing Alexandre to secure a position at 20 years of age at the Palais Royal of Louis-Philippe, Duke or Orléans.

Once in Paris, Dumas's glamorous life took flight. He started writing for popular magazines, and made a name for himself as a playwright before turning thirty. His success brought enough financial stability to let him take on writing full time and indulge in extensive travel. He also began a lifelong weakness for women, a weakness that followed him throughout his life, leaving, according to legend, over 40 mistresses and numerous illegitimate children behind. He did try marriage once, with actress Ida Ferrier in 1840.

Mid-stream during his playwriting career, Dumas changed course and began writing novels. At the time, serializations were extremely popular, so he took one of his plays and adapted it for installment reading. He also began a business to accommodate the insatiable market for serial adventure stories, hiring writers to churn out tales of intrigue. In addition, he produced several noteworthy non-fiction pieces, among them, *Celebrated Crimes,* an eight-volume collection addressing major European crime cases and criminals.

It is said that Dumas wrote published a total of 100,000 pages in his lifetime. Nonetheless, in spite of his enormous popularity and success, his biracial background was cause for prejudice. In 1843, he produced a novel entitled *Georges,* which dealt with issues such as race relations and colonialism.

His extravagant lifestyle drained his finances, and Dumas died in 1870 nearly broke. But his many tales of adventure live on, and have enjoyed a recent surge of popularity due to film and television adaptations. His writings, in particular his novels, have come to be considered much more complex than what they appear on the surface, as his themes take on large, complicated subjects such as the existence of God and Man's Search for Redemption. Much like his work, Alexandre Dumas will always be larger than life.

A Brief Synopsis

In 1815, Edmond Dantès, a handsome young sailor, appears to have everything at his fingertips: at only 19 years of age, he is poised to be made captain of a ship, the Pharaon (which he successfully docked in Marseilles after the death of its captain en route); he has a beautiful, engaging fiancée named Mercédès; and everyone who has the good fortune of coming into contact with him likes him tremendously. It's no surprise, then, that he is the object of envy among some of his peers, and even some of his supposed friends, each for his own specific reason: Danglars, the Pharaon's purser, envies Dantès' blossoming career; Fernand Mondego, who himself is in love with Dantès' fiancée, hates that he has her hand; Caderousse, an unscrupulous neighbor envies Dantès' luck; and Villefort, a prosecutor, fears that Dantès knows something that might jeopardize his career and social position.

Danglars, Mondego and Caderousse scheme a vengeful plan to stop Dantès in his tracks: they compile a letter accusing Dantès of treason, escalating a small, innocent act into a full-blown crime. Dantès, by request of his deceased captain, is in possession of a letter from Napoleon addressed to a group of Bonapartist sympathizers collected in Paris. He has no political agenda, but is simply doing his captain a favor; however, his involvement is enough to go forward with the charge, and on the day of his wedding, Dantès is arrested for treason. Villefort, the prosecutor, is initially skeptical of the accusations, recognizing them as fabricated and seeing no grounds for them other than envy. He believes that Dantès should be freed - that is, until he finds out to whom the letter was to be delivered: Villefort's own father, Noirtier. Upon this revelation, and the threat of having his father's political activities ruin his career, Villefort changes his position and joins in on the plan to imprison Dantès for life in order to keep him quiet. Monsieur Morrel, Dantès' superior and noble friend, intervenes on Dantès' behalf, but fails. Dantès is sent to Château d'If, a prison from which no one has ever been released or has escaped.

Dantès spends many horrible years at Château d'If in a small, hellish cell, slowly losing his mind. This downward spiral is broken by the sound of another prisoner, digging in a nearby cell. Dantès begins to dig as well, and finally meets the man who had broken his isolated silence, Abbé Faria. Faria, an Italian priest, is a long time political prisoner, and the two men strike a bond. An educator and intellectual, Faria teaches Dantès all the subjects of the sciences and humanities, including history, philosophy, literature and languages. He also alerts Dantès to the existence of a huge family fortune that rests on the island of Monte Cristo. He gives Dantès directions as to how to locate it should he ever be lucky enough to escape.

The men keep digging, but Faria cannot keep up the fight. Just as they are about to reach freedom, Faria dies. Dantès hides the priest's body and takes his robe for himself, making it into a sack and hiding within it. When the guards arrive to remove Faria's body, they are unaware that they are actually removing Dantès. The body is thrown out to sea, and Dantès is able to tear out of the sack, freeing himself.

Dantès immediately heads for Monte Cristo, where he finds the huge treasure that Faria told him would be there. Because of the treasure's enormity, he can't help but think that it is the manifestation of some kind of divine intervention: basically, God has granted him this gift in order for him to reward the good and decent people who tried to help him, while giving him the resources to also punish those who have mistreated him.

Now it is Dantès' turn to scheme.

Calling himself Abbé Busoni, and disguising himself as an Italian priest, Dantès returns travels to Marseilles. He seeks out Caderousse, who is now a struggling innkeeper. Caderousse confesses to the scheme to frame Dantès, then tells him that his father has died from a broken heart upon his incarceration, and that his former fiancée, Mercédès, is now married to Fernand Mondego. To makes matters even worse, both Danglars and Mondego have become wealthy, successful men and live in Parisian luxury. In gratitude for the updates, and for his remorse over his part in the scheme to frame him, Dantès gives Caderousse a diamond of great value. Dantès also saves his former friend Morrel from financial ruin, although he does so anonymously.

Ten years pass. Dantès is now is Rome, and goes by the title of Count of Monte Cristo. Forceful and determined, Dantès saves Albert de Morcerf, the son of Fernand Mondego and Mercédès, from being victimized by bandits. In return, Albert introduces Dantès to the most desirable social circles of Paris. Initially, no one recognizes Dantès, with one exception: Mercédès. Because he is the Count of Monte Cristo, Dantès begins to anonymously gain entry into the lives of Danglars, Mondego, and Villefort. Because he has spent the last ten years collecting enough information on each man to ruin them permanently, Dantès designs a vengeful plan to pay them back for the pain they caused him.

Mondego, also known as the Count de Morcerf, is Dantès' first victim. His first step is to expose the secret behind Morcerf's fortune: Morcerf had betrayed his business partner, Greek statesman Ali Pacha, later selling Pacha's wife and daughter, Haydée, into slavery. Dantès bought Haydée's freedom several years earlier, and from that time, she lived with him. Haydée testimony against Morcerf ruins his name and reputation, driving Albert and Mercédès to flee in shame. Morcerf sees no other option but to commit suicide.

Dantès' revenge against Villefort is more protracted and deliberate, occurring in steps as opposed to one sweeping act. First, Dantès manipulates Madame d'Villefort's proclivities towards murder and teaches her how to achieve her goals through poison. Madame d'Villefort begins to dispose of each member of Villefort's family. In the meantime, Dantès exposes Villefort's attempt to kill his illegitimate baby by burying the child alive. Villefort loses his mind, thinking that all is lost.

Danglars's greed is his own downfall, and Dantès uses this fault to bring down his former friend. He opens multiple bogus accounts with Danglars that nearly suck his finances dry. He also plays Danglars's adulterous wife, causing Danglars to lose even more money, and assists Eugénie, Danglers's daughter, is running out of town with a friend. At Danglars's lowest point, Dantès contracts an Italian criminal named Luigi Vampa to abduct Danglars and take whatever money he has left.

In contrast to all these acts of revenge, Dantès also seeks out ways to execute acts of kindness and generosity. He starts with Maximilian Morrel, the son of his ship-owner friend. Maximilian is engaged to Valentine Villefort, the stepdaughter of Madame d'Villefort, and is therefore vulnerable to her evil deeds. Dantès concocts a plan to save Valentine so that the couple could live "happily ever after." Much like Friar Lawrence's plan for Romeo and Juliet, Dantès gives Valentine a pill that simulates death. He then takes her away to the island of Monte Cristo. Maximilian, thinking that Valentine is dead, falls into a desperate depression. After a month, Dantès tells him that Valentine is, in fact, alive, and Maximilian embraces incomparable love. His tasks now complete, Dantès also finally finds love with the beautiful and loyal Haydée.

Characters

Edmond Dantès

The novel's protagonist and title character, Edmond Dantès is a man of honesty and decency. However, when he is unfairly framed and jailed for a crime he did not commit, resentment and bitterness overtake him. Upon his escape from jail, Dantès becomes wealthy and powerful, and believes that he must avenge the crimes against him by punishing those responsible, and rewarding the people who have helped him along the journey. His post-prison metamorphosis allows him to take on several alter egos in order to achieve his mission:

- The Count of Monte Cristo - Dantès takes on this title when he reaps the fortune promised to him which was found on the island of Monte Cristo. The Count is powerful and even cruel at times, and driven predominantly by his thirst for revenge.
- Lord Wilmore - This is the identity Dantès assumes – that of an unusual English nobleman – whenever he indulges in generous activities. Lord Wilmore's persona is diametrically opposed to that of the Count.
- Abbé Busoni - Dantès periodically takes on the guise of a priest for various reasons – sometimes to gain access that only a priest could, and other times to convince people, via priestly authority, to act the way he wants them to.
- Sinbad the Sailor - Dantès uses this name when he wants to keep a mysterious distance and paint himself a legend.

Mercédès

Dantès' beautiful fiancée, she is his equal in goodness and decency. She winds up married to one of Dantès' enemies, but never stops loving the young sailor of bygone days.

Abbé Faria

The intellectual priest and mentor who Dantès meets in prison. The Abbé becomes a father figure for Dantès, as he teaches him about arts and humanities while the men are incarcerated, likely saving Dantès' sanity. He also bequeaths Dantès his large treasure which is hidden on the island of Monte Cristo. If it weren't for Faria, there would be no Count of Monte Cristo.

Fernand Mondego

Mondego holds Dantès in contempt because he wants Mercédès, but she is in love with Dantès. As a result, he assists in the scheme to frame Dantès and send him to prison, allowing him to marry Mercédès himself. His conniving ways continue well afterwards, and he manages to gain great wealth and acquire the title of Count de Morcerf.

Baron Danglars

A greedy compadre of Fernand, Danglars is the mastermind behind the scheme to frame Dantès for treason. He, too, eventually becomes a wealthy and influential man, but winds up penniless after Dantès' revenge takes place.

Caderousse

The most inert of Dantès' enemies, Caderousse is lazy as well as avaricious. Unlike Danglars and Mondego, Caderousse never finds success and wealth but instead gets by from leading the life of a criminal.

Gérard d'Villefort

Villefort is the essence of ambition, but to a dangerous extent. A public prosecutor, he is actually responsible for Dantès' imprisonment, and as a result, is doomed to vengeful acts at the hands of Edmond.

Monsieur Morrel

Morrel is Dantès' boss when a sailor. Decent and kind, he does everything he can to get Dantès released from prison.

Louis Dantès

Dantès' father, Louis's grief over his son's imprisonment kills him.

Maximilian Morrel

The son of Monsieur Morrel, Maximilian shares his father's traits of goodness and decency. He and his love, Valentine, represent that which is good in people.

Albert de Morcerf

The son of Fernand Mondego and Mercédès, Albert has all the good traits of his mother and none of the bad of his father. His devotion to his mother is one of the things that affects the Count deeply and makes him question his mission.

Valentine Villefort

Villefort's innocent, beautiful, good and loving daughter, Valentine falls in love with Maximilian.

Noirtier

Villefort's elderly father, Noirtier was a, influential and powerful Bonapartist, and as such, is a perfect foil to his son's self-absorbed ambition.

Haydée

The daughter of Ali Pacha, who was the vizier Yanina, a Greek state. She and her mother are sold into slavery upon her father's murder, which was made possible by Fernand. Haydée is freed when Dantès buys her freedom (as the Count of Monte Cristo). He takes her with him, and she falls in love with him.

Signor Bertuccio

Dantès' servant (as the Count).

Benedetto

Villefort and Madame Danglars's illegitimate son, a product of their indiscretions. He becomes a criminal even though he was raised by kind adoptive parents who saved his life.

Madame d'Villefort

Villefort's greedy second wife, Madame d'Villefort does whatever it takes to secure her husband's fortune for her son, even criminal activity.

Julie and Emmanuel Herbaut

Julie, the lovely daughter of Monsieur Morrel and sister of Maximilian, and her kind and generous husband. They represent man's ability to be happy in this life even without material possessions. Instead, they have something better: love.

Madame Danglars

Danglars's philandering, greedy wife. Her antics and scheming help bring about her husband's eventual financial demise.

Eugénie Danglars

The Danglars's musically talented daughter. She wants to live the life of a bohemian artist, and runs away with her companion and soul mate, Louise d'Armilly, to do so.

Louise d'Armilly

Eugénie Danglars's music teacher, companion and most likely her true love.

Lucien Debray

The greedy lover of Madame Danglers, he works for the government and is therefore privy to inside information. He and Madame Danglars manipulate the stock market with her husband's money for high profits.

Ali

Dantès' mute Nubian slave.

Luigi Vampa

A legendary Roman bandit who was freed by Dantès. He is eternally indebted to him as a result.

Major Cavalcanti

A con artist whom Dantès (the Count) hires to portray an Italian nobleman.

Edward d'Villefort

The Villeforts's indulged son, Edward is an innocent victim of Dantès' mission of revenge.

Beauchamp

Journalist and friend to Albert de Morcerf.

Franz d'Epinay

Another good friend of Albert's, he is engaged for a time to Valentine, but does not want to be.

Marquis and Marquise of Saint-Méran

The parents of Villefort's first wife, murdered by the current Madame Villefort.

Jacopo

A smuggler who helps Dantès gain his freedom when he escapes prison.

Ali Pacha

Father to Haydée and a Greek nationalist leader betrayed by Mondego and, as a result, murdered.

Peppino

An Italian shepherd arrested as an accomplice to bandits after giving them food. Dantès/the Count buys his freedom.

Countess G—

A stunning Italian aristocrat who fears the Count of Monte Cristo, as she thinks he is a vampire.

Synopsis and Analysis

Chapters 1-5

Chapter 1: The Arrival at Marseilles

February, 1815: A crowd gathers at the port of Marseilles, excitedly anticipating the arrival of an impressive, three-masted ship called the Pharaon, owned by wealthy businessman Monsieur Morrel. Unfortunately, Morrel learns from Edmond Dantès, the ship's young, handsome first mate, that the ship's captain has died at sea; however, Dantès tells Morrel although they mourned their loss, the crew cooperated with him, allowing the rest of the journey to go well. Even more importantly, the cargo of the ship remained safe and retained its integrity. Morrel is taken with Dantès' ability to take charge, lead the crew and perform with utmost professionalism even at his young age of 19.

Danglars, the ship's purser who also harbors tremendous jealousy of Dantès, has another version of the journey. He tells Morrel that Dantès made a protracted stop at the Isle of Elba, which took them off schedule and detained them unnecessarily. Morrel confronts Dantès with Dangalrs' story, and Dantès explains to the businessman that he only made the stop to accommodate a last dying wish of the captain. The captain had asked Dantès to deliver a package to (grand-marshal) Maréchal Bertrand, who is exiled on Elba. He also added that while on the island, he encountered the deposed emperor, Napoleon.

Morrel accepts Dantès' version as the truth, and then asks the young man what he thinks of Danglers. With honest candor, Dantès tells him that, while he does not like him personally, Danglers's job performance is always admirable. Dantès' ability to not only speak with such honesty but also put aside his personal feelings further impresses Morrel, and he names the young first mate as the Pharaon's new captain. Dantès is thrilled and grateful; Danglars, however, becomes consumed with jealousy and envy over Dantès' good fortune.

Chapter 2: Father and Son

Dantès' first stop is his father's house. He is taken completely aback by the elder Dantès' failing health, and learns that the old man has not eaten properly for months. He then learns that Caderousse, a tailor, had forced the elder Dantès to pay a debt left by his son, leaving the old man with hardly any means to support himself. Dantès tells his father the about his promotion to captain, and gives him some gold to buy himself a new supply of food.

Caderousse joins the two Dantès men, welcoming young Dantès home and congratulating him on his promotion. Dantès acts civilly, and even though he knows what the tailor has done to his father, tries to let bygones be bygones and move forward. When Caderousse departs, he meets up with Danglars who had been waiting for him. The two men compare their distaste for Dantès, and agree that the young man has had too much come to him too easily. Caderousse, however, believes that the lucky streak may be ending soon, as he has heard that Mercédès, a young woman from the Catalans region and the love of Dantès' life, has been seeing another man in his absence. Danglars and Caderousse hope that this will result in something of a comeuppance, and camp outside Mercédès's home to see if the rumors of her betrayal are true.

Chapter 3: The Catalans

Dantès' next stop is Mercédès's house. He is surprised to find her cousin, Fernand Mondego, there with her. Fernand is also madly in love with Mercedes, and longs to marry her. When he arrives, Mercédès welcomes Dantès with enthusiastic affection, upsetting Fernand to the point that her leaves the house in a rage. Upon his departure, he comes upon Danglars and Caderousse, who are casually enjoying a bottle of wine. They invite Fernand to join them, and as the time passes, and the wine flows, the two men flame the fires of Fernand's jealousy over Dantès. Suddenly, Dantès and Mercédès are seen together, totally enamored of one another. They innocently announce their plans to marry the next day, as Dantès must depart for Paris to complete on last request of his former captain. Danglars, always suspicious, thinks that the trip has something to do with a delivery of a letter to Bonapartists in Paris, and the wheels of an evil plot of revenge to ruin Dantès once and for all are set into motion.

Chapter 4: The Plotters

Danglars and Fernand begin to contrive a plan designed to ruin Dantès; Caderousse, however, is too drunk to contribute. Fernand tells Danglers that he can never actually kill Dantès, as Mercedes has stated on many occasion that should something happen to Dantès, she would end her own life. Danglars offers the next best thing: imprisonment. He begins to compose a letter to the public prosecutor accusing Dantès of treason, being in possession of a letter from Napoleon to the Bonapartist sympathizers in Paris. Caderousse, in his stupor, objects to attacking Dantès' good name. Danglars then pretends that the idea was a joke, and throws the letter away. He then distracts Caderousse so that Fernand can retrieve the letter and send it on

Chapter 5: The Betrothal Feast

It is the wedding day of Dantès and Mercédès; however, in the middle of the joy and festivities, royal guards interrupt and arrest Dantès. No one can make sense of this turn of events, especially Dantès, who knows he is innocent. Morrel accepts Danglars's offer to act as captain of the Pharaon until Dantès is freed.

Analysis: Chapters 1 through 5

From the very beginning of *The Count of Monte Cristo,* the protagonist-hero, Edmond
Dantès, is depicted as a man of upstanding integrity, honesty and responsibility. Although still
only 19 years of age, he displays maturity beyond his years: he is a respected leader among his
crew, a devoted son to his father, and a loving and loyal partner to Mercedes. He is also a fair-
minded man, able to look beyond his personal reactions to people and evaluating them from a
point of neutrality. For example, when Morrel asks Dantès to give him his opinion on Danglars,
he puts his personal feelings aside and evaluates Danglars's good job performance objectively.
He applies this objectivity and sense of fairness to everyone else around him as well, securing his
posture as an admirable man.

On the other hand, Dantès' foils – Danglers, Caderousse and Fernand – are depicted as
weak and flawed men consumed with jealousy and a taste for revenge. They want to knock him
down, as they view him as unworthy and arrogant.

Danglers is the most dangerous of Dantès' enemies, as he is the smartest and most
conniving. He is fully aware of the ramifications the accusations of treason will carry, and
knows that the punishment will be severe. Still, his envy over Dantès' professional success
clouds his vision. Fernand's jealousy is based in passion. Because he wants Mercedes for
himself, he sees Dantès as an obstacle and wants to be rid of him. Finally, Caderousse is simply
a gullible follower, too weak to make his own decisions. Although he knows that Dantès is a
man of integrity, his fears prohibit him from defending the young sailor against Danglars's plot.
So each man has his own motivation to have Dantès stopped: Danglars's is his own ambition;
Fernand's is his irrational passion; and Caderousse's is his cowardice.

Chapters 6-14

Chapter 6: The Deputy Procureur

An aristocratic wedding is taking place between the daughter of the Marquis of Saint-
Méran and her fiancé, Gérard d'Villefort, the deputy public prosecutor of Marseilles. Villefort is
the son of a prominent Bonapartist; however, because of the emperor's defeat, Villefort believes
it to be in his best political interests to align himself with the royalists after the king, Louis
XVIII, has been reinstated. He becomes aggressively anti-Bonaparte, renouncing his own father
and dedicating himself to punishing anyone who sympathizes with the fallen emperor. The
wedding is halted when Villefort is called away to address an alleged, newly discovered
Bonapartist plot – the one involving Dantès and orchestrated by Danglars.

Chapter 7: The Examination

Morrel unsuccessfully tries to intervene on Dantès' behalf in response to his charge of treason. Villefort, in turn, confronts Dantès with the accusations. Dantès confesses that yes, he is in possession of a letter which was given to him by Napoleon. Still, he claims that he is innocent of a political agenda. He is simply living up to his promise to his dying captain. Dantès states that, for all intents and purposes, he has no loyalties except to his father, his girlfriend, and his sponsor, Monsieur Morrel.

Villefort responds to Dantès' sincerity. He is ready to dismiss the case until Dantès innocently reveals the recipient of the letter: Noirtier, who is not only Villefort's father but a die-hard Bonapartist. Villefort fears that his own political ambitions are now in jeopardy should his father's activities be revealed, and he banishes Dantès to prison.

Chapter 8: The Château D'If

Villefort orders that Dantès be imprisoned in the Château d'If, a prison known for being the place for only the most threatening political prisoners. Once he is there, Dantès demands to speak to the governor. When his request is denied, he threatens the guard, which lands him in the prison dungeon where the insane prisoners are incarcerated. The guard warns Dantès about one specific prisoner, a man who has apparently lost touch with reality and promises guards with monetary gifts in exchange for his freedom.

Chapter 9: The Evening of the Betrothal

Villefort returns to his fiancée's home telling her that he must depart for Paris. He confesses to his future father-in-law that if he can get to the monarch in time, he can save his fortune. En route, he meets Mercédès, who is trying to extract information about Dantès' whereabouts. Faced with the fact that he is responsible for annihilating the future of an innocent man in order to preserve his own success, Villefort is overcome with remorse and self-loathing.

Chapter 10: The Little Room in the Tuileries

In Paris, Villefort tells King Louis XVIII about the anti-monarch activities discussed in the letter Dantès was carrying. He warns the king of a real and dangerous conspiracy to resurrect Napoleon's reign.

Chapter 11: The Corsican Ogre

Villefort's warning is too late. Napoleon, already in France, is marching on Paris. Still, the king is grateful to Villefort for the warning, even though by now it means nothing.

Chapter 12: Father and Son

Noirtier visits Villefort, who tells him that the police are looking for a man who fits his profile and description regarding the murder of a royalist general. Noirtier shaves his beard and changes his clothes, hopping to deflect attention and suspicion. As he departs, he tells his son that the former emperor is gaining new momentum among his loyalists.

Chapter 13: The Hundred Days

The Emperor is victorious in conquering France in its entirety, and Bonapartism, obviously, is no longer a criminal offense. In an attempt to intervene on Dantès' behalf, Monsieur Morrel contacts Villefort several times, but with no success, given Villefort's personal desire to keep Dantès imprisoned. Danglars, however, doesn't know Villefort's secret, and therefore is afraid that Dantès will not only be freed but also come after him. To guard his own safety, he leaves his position with Morrel and flees to Spain. Meanwhile, Fernand has become confidante to Mercédès. She is grateful for his attention, but it comes to an end when he leaves to serve in Napoleon's army.

Dantès' father, distraught and despondent over his son's jailing, dies from a broken heart and spirit. Monsieur Morrel pays for his funeral. In yet another political upheaval, Napoleon is deposed after only three and a half months. Louis XVIII once again takes his place on the throne.

Chapter 14: In the Dungeons

The inspector-general of prisons visits Dantès at the Château d'If. The young captain makes his plea for a fair trial, and the inspector responds positively. He tells Dantès that he will do what he can. But, when he learns that, according to Villefort, Dantès was in concert with the Bonapartists and may have been instrumental in Napoleon's return to France, he removes himself from the case and tells Dantès that there is nothing he can do.

Analysis: Chapters 6 through 14

Along with introducing the characters and storyline, the first few chapters of the book depict the political dichotomy which existed in 19th century France, that being, the posture of the Bonapartists, who supported the Emperor's position on liberal, democratic principles, versus the more old-school, conservative Royalists who vehemently stood by the traditions of the throne.

Dumas also designs camps for his characters, with each camp being represented: Morrel, Dantès, his deceased captain, and Noirtier (liberals), and Villefort and the Marquise de Saint-Méran, among others, Royalists. Moreover, the Royalists are drawn as unsympathetic characters – selfish, greedy and self-serving – while the liberals are, for all intents and purposes, noble and ethical. Given that Dumas himself was a great supporter of Napoleon's posture (possibly due to his own father's history as a general in the Emperor's army), the clear contrast between these camps is expected. The author was raised in a household that held the rights of the individual in the highest esteem, and his writing is heavily laden with the ideals that are most closely associated with Napoleon as opposed to the antiquated, prejudiced views of the Royalists.

The first section of *The Count of Monte Cristo* also reflects on the less philosophical and more realistic political condition of 19th century France, that being, where anything or anyone viewed as a potential threat to the post-revolutionary state is systematically eliminated. For example, Dantès' individual rights are unduly placed in jeopardy due to Villefort's ambition; Noirtier describes a political system where the ideas behind a regime reign supreme over the good of the people; and men of character are seen as roadblocks to the progress of the political machine. Dantès, as such as man, finds himself in the difficult role of savior, standing up for what is intrinsically good and then suffering the consequences of his courage.

Another popular movement that Dumas addresses is that of Romanticism. Dantès, being a man motivated by feelings over intellect, serves as a Romantic hero – that is, until later in the book when he reinvents himself as the Count of Monte Cristo. By then, he has suffered more and, as a result, fallen away from the ideals of the movement. It is interesting to note that the farther he detaches himself from the Romantic viewpoint, the less his character is respected and/or respectable. His taste for revenge replaces his ability to feel sympathy or empathy for others, and he loses his way. Again, Dumas imposes his own beliefs on Romanticism as the ideal posture.

Readers often comment on the fact that chapters 2 and 12 share a subtitle: Father and Son. The author once again draws a contrast between scenarios, this time between, as the title suggests, fathers and sons, specifically Louis and Edmond Dantès versus Noirtier and Villefort. The Dantès men share a loving bond, with each one consistently placing the well-being of the other above his own. Noirtier and Villefort, on the other hand, share little beyond suspicion of one another. Even worse, Villefort is prepared to do whatever it takes, even denouncing his father and his name, to better his own lot. Dantès is loyal and kind; Villefort is scheming and ruthless. Their characters are as diametrically opposed as their relationships with their fathers, so the shared chapter subtitle is rooted in irony.

Chapters 15-20

Chapter 15: Number 34 and Number 27

Dantès finds solace in religion during his first six years as a prisoner, with prayer being a focal point of his existence. But as the years pass and he reflects on his situation, his faith turns to despair and anger. He is overwhelmed, and contemplates suicide to put an end to his suffering when he hears scratching sounds from an adjacent wall. Curious, he contrives a way to learn more: when his dinner is delivered, he strategically places his dish where he knows it will be stepped on by the guard. As a result, he is left the entire pot of food, and he uses the pot's handle as a tool to help him explore the origin of the sounds. He scrapes the wall for hours on end until finally, he breaks through and discovers a prison mate on the other side.

Chapter 16: A Learned Italian

Dantès' mate identifies himself as Abbé Faria, a political rebel who supports a unified Italy. Before long, he realizes that the Abbé is the same priest that he has heard the guard speak of as crazed. Dantès is thrilled to have discovered another human being to communicate with; the abbé, on the other hand, was hoping that their efforts would have yielded an escape tunnel, not a friendship.

Chapter 17: In the Abbé's Cell

Faria, Dantès learns, is not crazy, but instead, is a highly intelligent, educated man. Even though in prison, he found a way to construct useful tools such as pens and ink, and write a political discourse. He also constructed sharper tools which he used to scrape his tunnel towards Dantès' cell. When the young captain tells Faria his tale of woe, the abbé deduces that Dantès was set up by his so-called friends, Danglars and Fernand. Being a political figure himself, Faria also draws the relationship between Villefort and Noirtier, solving the question as to what motivated Villefort's actions. After hearing all these explanations, Dantès is filled with a taste for vengeance.

The abbé begins Dantès on a new educational journey, teaching him about a diverse spectrum of subjects including mathematics, languages and philosophy. Dantès is a very quick study, and catches on with ease, which pleases his tutor. Faria begins strategizing a new escape, and Dantès decides to help; however, before they can execute the plan, Faria falls ill. It appears as if he has had a stroke, as he can no longer move the right side of his body. Days before they are going to put the plan into action, however, Faria suffers a fit. Dantès refuses to leave without him.

Chapter 18: The Treasure

The following day, Faria tells Dantès about a hidden treasure that once belonged to the

House of Spada, one of Italy's wealthiest families. Dantès begins to wonder if the rumors about the Abbé's mental instability are actually true. But the old man insists, and little by little, Dantès is convinced that he is speaking the truth.

According to Faria, back in the 15ᵗʰ century, Caesar Spada took the family treasure to an island called Monte Cristo in an attempt to keep it out of reach from a conniving, deceitful and greedy pope. Somehow, the exact location of where Caesar hid the treasure was lost, even to the remaining members of the Spada family. That is, until Faria learned where it was by deciphering a secret, coded message. While employed as the private secretary to the sole survivor of the Spada bloodline, he unraveled the mystery behind the treasure's whereabouts.

Upon Spada's death, Faria inherited everything he owned, which, technically, included the treasure. And now, because Faria considers Dantès his adopted son, he, too, has a right to the treasure by association. Faria gives Dantès a document which states exactly where to find this elusive treasure on the uninhabited island of Monte Cristo.

Chapter 19: The Death of the Abbé

In order to ensure its safety, Faria makes Dantès memorize the map and directions to the treasure. Days later, Faria suffers another attack, this time fatal. He dies.

Chapter 20: The Cemetery of the Château d'If

Faria's death destroys Dantès emotionally. He cannot bring himself to leaving his friend's body, which is shrouded in fabric, waiting to be removed for burial. His anguish breaks when an idea strikes him: Dantès decides to switch places with the corpse, thus allowing him an escape from the prison. Cutting Faria's body out from the shroud, he then brings it to his cell, then returns to sew himself into the shroud. Assuming that the body will be buried in the ground, he takes a knife to dig himself out. When the prison guards arrive later to remove Faria's body, Dantès, lying still and quiet, is taken instead, steps away from freedom. However, instead of a ground burial, they tie a cannonball to the "corpse" and toss it into the sea.

Analysis: Chapters 15 through 20

The first chapter in this section, Chapter 15, is entitled "Number 34 and Number 27." Dumas chose this title to reflect what he considered another crime against humanity, or, more specifically in live with hid democratic posture, a threat to individualism. While imprisoned, Dantès and Faria are stripped of any individual human attributes, and are instead regarded as nothing more than property – numbered instead of named. The absence of a name symbolizes the absence of self, of rights, of a voice or position in the world.

Ironically, it is another prisoner, Faria, who assists Dantès in regaining his self-worth. Their relationship restores their own humanity, as they treat one another with respect. They engage in intelligent conversation, explore intellectual thoughts and fight to retain their humanity together. In essence, they save one another's sanity.

Dumas presents Abbé Faria as an archetype of the 18th century: a thoughtful, educated philosopher navigating a world that lacks appreciation for the contributions and emotional capacity of individuals. The education he imparts to Dantès, in spite of their surroundings, gives the young captain the strength of will to be true to his individualism and nature.

When Faria figures out the whys and hows behind Dantès' incarceration, it marks the beginning of Dantès' metamorphosis from an idealistic, life-affirming young man to one filled with vengeance and hate. (The fact that Dantès was unable to figure out what his enemies were doing on his own speaks to his character and naiveté.) Upon going to prison, he is still hopeful that all will be resolved and he will be freed; however, once he learns the truth from the Abbé, the old Dantès is replaced with a new man – one whose actions are now dictated solely by revenge, so much so that it renders him incapable of embracing life's happier aspects and joys. The weight of the truth is almost too much for him to bear. Even when he hears about the Spada treasure – a treasure that Faria tells him is now his – he can only absorb it from the vantage point of how it can help him get back at those who have harmed him. It never enters his mind how much freedom and happiness it might bring.

The metaphor of prison as a kind of death permeates this section of the book. Dumas uses descriptively morbid language, driving home the point that the prison is like an emotional, intellectual, spiritual and, of course, physical, tomb. But it begs the question: does the tomb encase Dantès? Does it represent the end of innocence? Or, on a much larger scale, does it signal the end of man's ability to sympathize, or even more, empathize with his fellow man? Just how much has Dantès, and man, lost, and can it ever be recovered?

Chapters 21-25

Chapter 21: The Isle of Tiboulen

Dantès cuts himself loose, releasing himself from the shroud. He then begins to figure out which way to swim, and heads for an island he recalls from his time at sea, finally reaching it in an exhausted state. As he gains composure while resting on the island's coastal rocks, a storm hits. He sees a small boat fall victim to the storm, crashing against the rocks. There are no survivors. Next, he spies a ship from Genoa that lingers afar. He decides that this ship is his only chance for true survival. He confiscates a cap from one of the soldiers who perished on the small boat, then grabs a log of driftwood to use as a float, and drifts towards the ship. Once there, he tells the Genoese sailors that he was the only one to survive the small boat's crash and asks for help. The sailors are suspicious – Dantès looks like the long time prisoner that he is, what with hair and beard unkempt; however, he manages to make an excuse that his hair is a symbol of religious devotion. The sailors accept his explanation and allow him onboard.

Chapter 22: The Smugglers

Before long, Dantès realizes that the Genoese ship is one carrying smugglers. Still, he ingratiates himself to them for his own purposes. Soon enough, she ship comes upon the island of Monte Cristo to, allegedly, transact an illegal deal.

Chapter 23: The Isle of Monte Cristo

Once on Monte Cristo, Dantès feigns an injury. He tells his shipmates that he cannot leave with them, and for them to comeback for him in a week. Dantès' best mate, Jacopo, suggest that he stay on the island, even if it means losing his share of the transaction. Dantès is touched by his offer, but refuses.

Chapter 24: The Search

Dantès is alone on Monte Cristo, is thusly begins looking for the treasure. He succeeds, and is thrown by the enormity of its worth. Dantès drops to the ground, thanking God for his good fortune.

Chapter 25: At Marseilles Again

The sailors return for Dantès, and they head for Leghorn. Upon arrival, Dantès sells a few of the precious gems from the treasure which he placed in his pockets prior to them coming back for him. From the monies he receives from the sale of some diamonds, he purchases a boat and crew for Jacopo in gratitude for his friendship. In return, he asks Jacopo to go to Marseilles and seek out one Louis Dantès, and a young woman named Mercédès.

Dantès then leaves the smugglers and buys a large boat for himself. He sails back to Monte Cristo and hides the treasure in a secret compartment of the vessel. Several days later. his friend Jacopo returns to Monte Cristo with bad news: Louis Dantès has died, and the whereabouts of Mercédès is unknown. Dantès sails to Marseilles himself, a broken man from the news.

Analysis: Chapters 21 through 25

Dantès' imprisonment was equated to death; now, his escape symbolizes a resurrection. Even his escape echoes a baptism, taking place underwater. Dantès is now a man with one objective in mind: revenge. He has convinced himself that he is entitled, and that God wills it.

Dantès' metamorphosis is immediately apparent: an honest man, he now lies without conflict or remorse, especially to the smugglers. He has changed completely, with little of the former Dantès in view. When he finally finds the treasure, he considers it a mixed blessing: the fortune will allow him to complete his task, which is a gift; however, the task is steeped in misery, that being, revenge. In order to achieve it, he must set aside all his former human decency and singularly concentrate on the task ahead: annihilating his enemies. He looks to God for support in this unsavory mission, convincing himself that divine will is on his side. Why else would God have led him to the treasure? And on an island named "Monte Cristo," or "Mountain of Christ," no less? Whether God's approval is imaginary or not, Dantès believes that his objectives are legitimate. He forges ahead to realize them.

Chapters 26-30

Chapter 26: The Inn of Pont Du Gard

Dantès, now disguised as an Italian priest and calling himself "Abbé Busoni," journeys to an inn which is owned by his old acquaintance, Caderousse, and his wife, who is gravely ill. He finds them financially destitute. He passes himself off as the executor of Dantès' will, and tells them that Dantès acquired a valuable diamond while in prison. According to "Abbé Busoni," Dantès' last request was that the diamond be divided among his most beloved friends and family: his father, Caderousse, Danglars, Fernand, and Mercédès.

Chapter 27: The Tale

Caderousse wants exclusive possession of the jewel, and tries to contrive a way of achieving that. He exposes the series of events which led to Dantès' arrest and imprisonment, which perfectly matched Faria's theory. Caderousse voices his regrets, and Dantès/Abbé Busoni accepts his confession. He gives Caderousse the whole diamond.

Caderousse fills Dantès/Abbé Busoni in on what has happened to the rest of his friends. Danglars fled to Spain, worked for a bank, and wound up a powerful millionaire now living in Paris; Fernand is now also rich and influential, but how he got them remains nebulous; and Mercédès, believing Dantès to be dead, married Fernand. They, too, now live in Paris. Caderousse also tells Dantès/Abbé Busoni that Louis Dantès expired from a broken heart. Morrel and Mercédès offered him solace and a place to stay, but he remained inconsolable. Morrel even offered Louis money, and gave him a red silk purse filled with gold. Caderousse now has possession of this purse, and Dantès asks for it.

Caderousse continues to explain that Morrel is now nearly bankrupt. With the exception of the Pharaon, his ships have sunk. and he can't pay off his creditors. Caderousse asks the Abbé why bad things happen to good people. Dantès/Abbé Busoni tells him that this isn't true, and to have faith.

Chapter 28: The Prison Registers

Time for his next disguise.

Pretending to an English representative of Thomson and French, an investment firm, Dantès goes to the office of the mayor of Marseilles. The mayor has considerable investments in Morrel's business, as does the inspector of prisons, whose investments are even larger. Dantès buys the prison inspector's stakes at full value. He then asks to see the prison records for Abbé Faria, stating that he had been Faria's pupil. With access to Faria's records, Dantès takes the opportunity to peruse his own. He steals the accusatory document that Danglars composed and Fernand delivered, and validates that Villefort ordered his incarceration.

Chapter 29: The House of Morrel and Son

Still disguised as the representative of Thomson and French, Dantès next goes to Morrel, who is devastated by his impending financial ruin. He currently has only two men on payroll, one of whom is a twenty-three-year-old clerk, Emmanuel Herbaut, who is in love with his daughter, Julie. Morrel needs to pay his creditors in a matter of days, but has no money to do so.

While Dantès is still in Morrel's office, they learn the dreaded news that the *Pharaon* has been lost. Dantès, who now owns a significant percentage of Morrel's debt, grants him amnesty in the form of an extra three months to make the payment. As he exits, Dantès tells Julie to follow any instructions she receives from someone calling himself "Sinbad the Sailor."

Chapter 30: The Fifth of September

The three months Dantès granted Morrel are closing in, and the businessman still has no money. He makes the decision that ending his life is better than the humiliation of his debt. Morrel shares his plan with his son, Maximilian, who supports his father's decision. Meanwhile, Julie gets a letter from Sinbad the Sailor. She follows the instructions he has sent her, leading her to the red silk purse Morrel once gave to Louis Dantès. Inside, she finds her father's debt notes, all marked as paid. The purse also holds an enormous diamond, specified for Julie so that she can marry Emmanuel.

Just as Morrel is about to shoot himself, Julie arrives with the good news. Commotion ensues outside, where they see a ship docking. It is an exact replica of the Pharaon, only flush with cargo. Satisfied with the happy events, Dantès boards his boat and departs Marseilles.

Analysis: Chapters 26 through 30

Judging by his language, it is obvious that Dantès sees himself as a divine agent, having received his fortune from God. This is underlined further by his choice of disguises: a priest. He clearly believes himself to be God's messenger, even in his quest for revenge.

Dantès' various disguises reflect what he sees as his specific roles: he is the Abbé Busoni when visiting Caderousse, as he is in a position of judgment; he is an English investment officer (later called Lord Wilmore) when acting in generosity towards Morrel; and he is Sinbad the Sailor when acting in an unusual fashion. Dantès, believing himself to be acting according to God's will, appoints each aspect to his personality its own unique identity.

Among all his names, Sinbad the Sailor is the most recognizable. A character in a Middle Eastern folktale, Sinbad is a traveling merchant who ultimately finds enormous wealth. There are certainly parallels between Dantès and Sinbad: each is a sailor, each faces multiple journeys, and each winds up wealthy; however, a deeper explanation for this name involves the porter character in the Sinbad tale who covets the sailor's fortune and resents his own lot in life. By the end of the story, the porter actually comes to appreciate his so-called boring existence, when he compares it to the trial, tribulations and dangers Sinbad faces. Just like the porter, Dantès' friends resent his good fortune, and attack him because of it; but when the tables are turned, Dantès, or "Sinbad the Sailor," punishes them for their greed and envy.

And what of the red silk purse? The bag is a symbol for kindness, generosity and reward for good deeds. Morrel first used it to help Louis Dantès; Dantès uses it to reciprocate Morrel's kindness to his father by rewarding Morrel's daughter. Still, it can be argued that on some level, Dantès wants Morrel to recognize who is truly orchestrating this act of generosity. He would have to guess that Morrel would recognize the purse as the one he gave to Louis. As a result, he would make the connection that leads to Dantès being Julie's benefactor. This slightly diminishes Dantès' motives, as what defines true acts of altruism is anonymity.

Chapters 31-34

Chapter 31: Italy: Sinbad the Sailor

Ten years have passed since Dantès went to Marseilles in disguise to set his plans into motion. Back at Monte Cristo, a young Parisian aristocrat, Baron Franz d'Epinay, arrives to go on a hunt for wild goats. Franz encounters a group of men, and from their manner, assumes that they are smugglers; however, he soon learns that they are actually the yacht crew of a wealthy resident of the island who is strangely referred to as Sinbad the Sailor. Sinbad, supposedly, travels the world at the drop of a hat, and the crew is always ready to accommodate him.

They bring Franz to meet the mysterious man at his luxurious home – or palace, really – which rests hidden behind the island's rocky terrain. Franz, in spite of his own wealth and standing, is rendered speechless at the sight of Sinbad's opulence. Sinbad, who is actually Dantès, shares with Franz his lifestyle of constant travel. During these travels, he also often comes upon opportunities to perform random acts of philanthropy, which is indulges. He has even been known to spare the lives of so-called criminals and bandits. He goes on to tell Franz the story of how he first encountered his own slave, a mute Nubian he calls Ali. According to the story, Ali was found in Tunis, in too close proximity to the harem of the king. His punishment was to have his tongue, then his hand and finally his head, dismembered. Hearing this sentence, Sinbad waited for the slave's tongue to be cut out, then bought him for himself, sparing his life. The conversation then takes a whole different direction as Sinbad begins to glorify and rave about the benefits of hallucinogenic drugs. The two men eventually take some together, and Franz has a dramatic, realistic "trip" like nothing he has experienced before.

Chapter 32: The Awakening

When morning breaks, Franz tries to access Sinbad's hidden grotto, but fails. He leaves for Rome, where he meets up with his friend, Viscount Albert de Morcerf, the son of Fernand Mondego, now the Count de Morcerf. They plan to stay in Rome for the annual pre-Lenten carnival, but need to rent a coach in order to fully enjoy it; however, none are available.

Chapter 33: Roman Bandits

The hotel's proprietor tells Franz and Albert to be aware of Roman bandits, especially during the carnival. He warns them of one specific, famous bandit, a man named Luigi Vampa. The young men find the warnings a bit fantastical, and are reluctant to believe them. But the proprietor fills them in on Vampa's history: he had been a peaceful young shepherd with a love for life, art, and love for a shepherdess called Teresa. One day, a notorious bandit named Cucumetto accidentally encountered Vampa and Teresa as he was racing away from capture by the police. They hid Cucumetto in spite of the fact that a large reward had been promised to anyone who could assist in his capture.

Chapter 34: Vampa

The story continues, with Teresa in attendance at a luxurious party, dancing with an aristocrat and admiring the beautiful gown the hostess was wearing. As Vampa watched her dance, he was overcome with jealousy. In an attempt to win her attention, he promised her that he would somehow get her the gown. That night, he torched the home of the host, and stole the gown in the midst of the confusion. The next day, as Teresa was putting on the gown, a lost traveler approached Vampa for directions. The traveler, calling himself Sinbad the Sailor, gave Vampa two precious stones for his help. Just as Vampa returned to Teresa, he found her in the process of being kidnapped. After killing the perpetrator, he learned that he had actually killed Cucumetto. Vampa stole Cucumetto's clothing, put them on, and went to the band of bandits to declare himself their new leader.

Analysis: Chapters 31 through 34

During the decade that passed between Dantès' trip to Marseilles and the meeting between him and Franz, Dantès has truly transformed into the dazzling, mysterious, almost supernatural Count of Monte Cristo. Dumas gives the reader very few details about how the transformation actually took place, save for some stories here and there about his elusive presence. This only adds to the Count's mystery in intrigue. What is, however, conveyed, is that the Count lives a life that barely compares to a normal existence on any level. He has traveled the world, and encountered experiences that legends are made of. Dumas draws the Count as a man who can do almost anything, even beyond human capabilities. He is daring, cunning, glamorous, dangerous, strong and even magical. Even his physicality is described by the author is terms that hint at the supernatural. He is unrecognizable from the young, idealistic and loving sea captain that emerged at the start of the novel.

Monte Cristo is a walking dichotomy: his life is obviously one of luxury, but he does not seem inclined to indulge in it himself. He has sumptuous food available, but rarely eats. There are beautiful women available to him, yet he is aloof and uninterested. So although he is constantly surrounded by every possible physical luxury and pleasure, he spends all his time – every waking hour – plotting and seeking revenge. His only escape is hallucinogens, for they allow him to shut down his dark thoughts, at least temporarily.

The Count's obsession with drugs reflects the times, particularly the posture of the Romantic period. The Romantic fascination with hallucinogens ties in with its preoccupation with feelings, and their elevated status when compared to mere intellect. Hallucinogens opened the door to new sensory experiences, and thusly, new feelings which could complement one's emotional connection to and understanding of the world. They could also propel a certain kind of emotional transcendence – one that went beyond the limits of everyday existence. This ability to transcend was a goal of the Romantics, and Dumas's mention of drug-induced experiences taps into the Romantic mind-set of the times.

Chapters 35-39

Chapter 35: The Colosseum

Franz is still in Rome. One day, he goes to visit the Colosseum and accidentally overhears a conversation between the Count of Monte Cristo host (Dantès) and Luigi Vampa, the famous bandit about whom his hotel proprietor told him. They are discussing the situation of a shepherd called Peppino, who has been falsely arrested for being a bandit accomplice. Peppino's only crime has been bringing the bandits some food; however, he has nonetheless been sentenced to a beheading, scheduled to occur in 48 hours in a public square. The Count tells Vampa that he will arrange for Peppino's release by buying his freedom; Vampa, in turn, pledges his allegiance to the Count.

The next night, Franz and his friend Albert go to the opera house. Once again, Franz is surprised to find the Count there as well, this time, accompanied by Haydée, whose beauty take Franz's breath away. A Greek, she is dressed in a Greco-inspired ensemble. The equally beautiful "Countess G—," who is sitting with Franz and Albert, is filled with fear at the sight of the Count, whom she believes to be a vampire, judging from his complexion and manner. In the morning, the hotel proprietor tells the young men that another guest, the Count of Monte Cristo, has made his coach available to them for the carnival. Albert and Franz go to the island, and are flabbergasted by the revelation that Franz's weird, elusive host when he visited the island for the goat hunt and the Count of Monte Cristo are in fact one in the same.

Chapter 36: La Mazzolata

The Count asks his two young guests to join him in witnessing a public execution that is to take place. He also tells them of his unorthodox interest in such things. The three men begin an exchange on justice.

As the execution is about to commence, one of the two men accused, Peppino, is suddenly released, while the other is executed in a grisly fashion. Monte Cristo watches, never losing composure. He is creepily engrossed in the act of vengeance in front of him.

Chapter 37: The Carnival at Rome

Albert's goal is to have many "liaisons" with as many women during the 72 hour carnival. He is seen flirting with a certain beautiful women, but does not intend to limit his conquests to her.

Chapter 38: The Catacombs of Saint Sebastian

The beautiful woman with whom Albert is flirting is Vampa's mistress, Teresa. Albert is actually being entrapped, and Vampa swoops in to kidnap him. Franz is delivered a ransom note via Peppino, but knows he cannot pay it. He goes to the Count for help. Peppino takes Franz and the Count to the bandits' hideout, which is in the Catacombs of Saint Sebastian. When Vampa sees the Count, he greets him like a friend. He immediately releases Albert and apologizes to the Count for the misunderstanding. Albert sees the whole experience as surreal, but thanks the Count nonetheless for his freedom.

Chapter 39: The Rendezvous

As an act of gratitude for saving his life, The Count of Monte Cristo asks Albert to introduce him to Parisian society when he plans to be in the city. Albert is happy to oblige. Franz, however, is less so, and much less enchanted with the Count as his friend. For instance, he makes note of how the Count almost trembles when he shakes hands with Albert. He goes on to warn Albert about the conversation he overheard at the Colosseum as well. The act has the opposite effect in that it only heightens Albert's attraction to the Count.

Analysis: Chapters 35 through 39

Travel writing was an extremely popular genre in the 19th century, and Dumas himself was an accomplished travel writer before he turned to novels – a fact that is evident in this section. He creates an exceptionally vivid portrait of Italy, exploring its culture and traditions as well as the many ways it differed from France. Dumas paints a much more sensual place in Italy, filled with an earthy intrigue and love for life, while also depicting its more sophisticated side through art and entertainment such as the opera. To his French audience, Italy was almost considered exotic by comparison.

Dumas also indulges France's preoccupation with all things Greek, initially through his introduction of Haydée. Greece held great interest to French writers of the time due to its fight for independence from Great Britain in the 1820s. By taking his readers to a variety of locations, through reference, influence and imagery, Dumas not only showcases his own talents as a travel writer buy also indulges the audience's taste for descriptive tales in alluring places.

Countess G—'s fear that the Count is a vampire reflects another archetypical fascination associated with Romanticism, that being, tales of horror. Countess G— repeatedly refers to the Count as "Lord Ruthven," who was the protagonist of a popular 1816 story entitled "The Vampyre." Though "The Vampyre" was written by Dr. John William Polidari, it was often erroneously credited to the famous Romantic poet Lord Byron, which broadened its readership. Charles Nodier also wrote a drama based on Lord Ruthven, and Dumas wrote another soon after. The Romantic interest in horror, in vampires in particular, reached its apex upon the publication of Bram Stoker's *Dracula* in 1897. Much like the Count of Monte Cristo, Lord Ruthven was depicted as both intriguing and frightening.

The discussion on human justice that breaks out among the Count, Franz, and Albert addresses various issues which align with the Count's plan for revenge. He voices his frustration over guilty people often being set free, even after horrendous acts of violence. He then continues by saying that for those who do receive punishment, the punishment is not severe enough. In other words, the criminal should suffer as much as his victims did and do, which is the kind of revenge the Count has in mind for his enemies. He will destroy them on all fronts: physically, emotionally, psychologically and spiritually.

The character of Albert is given consideration in this section. First seen as a reckless youth looking only for a good time, there are signs of what he is to become as the novel continues, particularly in his brave reaction to his kidnapping rescue by the Count. He has the makings of a man of maturity.

Finally, who is Countess G? Some argue that this was simply the author's way, as other writers have also done, to keep the story rather than the names of characters center stage. (Franz Kafka, for one, used this conceit quite often.) Other scholars think that it was Dumas's way of maintaining the privacy of aristocracy, who were often the inspiration for his characters. But most scholars and readers alike think it is a reference to Countess Teresa Guiccioli, the mistress of Lord Byron, who himself is mentioned throughout the book.

Chapters 40-46

Chapter 40: The Guests

The Count of Monte Cristo heads to Paris, and to Albert's home. Albert, excited to be the reciprocal host, invites some of his friends over for breakfast to meet the mysterious man, including Lucien Debray, the secretary to the Minister of the Interior, and Beauchamp, a journalist.

Chapter 41: The Breakfast

Before long, an additional two guests arrive - the Baron of Château-Renaud, a diplomat, and Maximilian Morrel, now a French army captain. Not only did Maximilian save Château-Renaud's life in Constantinople, he also did it on the anniversary of his father's fortuitous financial turnaround. Since that day, he made a vow to always perform an act of kindness on that day in honor of its significance and in gratitude for his father's good fortune.

The Count is the perfect guest, captivating all of Albert's friends and acquaintances with his stories of travel and intrigue, including the one about Luigi Vampa, where he captured the bandit and made him vow to never harm anyone in the Count's favor. His own attentions, however, are focused on Maximilian.

Chapter 42: The Presentation

After breakfast, the guests depart. Albert then gives the Count a tour of his house. He shows the Count a portrait of his mother, which his father despises. She is seen in Catalan clothing, specifically those of a fisherwoman, and is gazing upon the ocean's coast.

Albert then introduces the Count to his parents. Fernand, who is now a senator, has no clue of the Count's true identity, but Mercédès recognizes him immediately. Frightened for their safety, she warns her son to be careful in his new friend's company.

Chapter 43: Monsieur Bertuccio

The Count of Monte Cristo buys a summer home in Auteuil. The previous owner was the Marquis of Saint-Méran, whose daughter died soon after marrying Villefort.

Chapter 44: The House at Auteuil

The Count goes to visit his new retreat at Auteuil. As he surveys the property, his steward, Bertuccio, becomes uncontrollably agitated. When the Count asks him what is behind the outburst, he begins to tell a complicated story.

Chapter 45: The Vendetta

Years earlier, Bertuccio's his brother, who was a soldier in Napoleon's army, was murdered in Nîmes by assassins loyal to the throne. In a quest for justice, Bertuccio went to the public prosecutor of Nîmes, Gérard d'Villefort. Villefort, being a royalist, had no time for Bertuccio's plight and ignored his request, filling Bertuccio with his own thirst for revenge.

Villefort became aware of Bertuccio's anger and thus feared for his own safety. He had hoped that his transfer to Versailles would distance him from Bertuccio, but Bertuccio followed him there. Bertuccio soon found out that Villefort spent many nights at the house in Auteuil (the same house the Count had just purchased), holding clandestine meetings with his mistress. On one of these nights, Bertuccio waited patiently in the garden for Villefort, and upon seeing him, attacked him with a dagger, and believed him to be dead. Prior to Bertuccio's attack, Villefort buried a mysterious box, which Bertuccio grabbed, thinking it was a treasure. It was, instead, a dying baby, barely able to breathe. After mouth-to-mouth resuscitation, the baby regained its ability to breathe, and was taken to the hospital, where it stayed for several months. When able, Bertuccio took the baby to his home, and he and his widowed sister-in-law raised it.

Bertuccio and his sister-in-law named him Benedetto. The child was a bad seed from the start, always getting into trouble. Once he was old enough, he left home and never contacted his adopted family. As time went on, Bertuccio was smuggling goods into France. On one occasion, as he was fleeing from the authorities, he hid in a loft behind Caderousse's inn and was witness to a hideous scene: Caderousse and his wife had asked a jeweler to buy the diamond that the Abbé Busoni had given them. The jeweler gave the couple 45,000 francs for the diamond, and then asked for a room, as the weather had taken a bad, stormy turn.

Chapter 46: The Rain of Blood

Once Caderousse had his hands on the 45,000 francs, he didn't want to share it or the diamond. He murdered both the jeweler and his own wife, leaving with the money and the diamond, doubling his profits.

When the police arrived, they arrested Bertuccio for the crime. Bertuccio told them of a priest named Abbé Busoni, who had supposedly given Caderousse the diamond in the first place. The police began searching for the priest, and when he finally showed up, he visited Bertuccio in the prison. Bertuccio shared his unbelievable story with the abbé, and the priest told him that when he is released, to find the Count of Monte Cristo, who would give him a position as a steward. Caderousse eventually resurfaced and confessed, allowing Bertuccio to be released. Caderousse was sentenced to a lifetime of hard labor.

When he was eleven years of age, Benedetto came home. With Bertuccio away on a job, the boy tortured his mother for a pittance of money, eventually killing her.

Analysis: Chapters 40 through 46

Drama dominates this novel, reflecting Dumas's background as a playwright. The plot is almost always advanced through dialogue: it explains the Count's relationship with Vampa; Maximilian's courage and fortitude; and Mercédès's recognition of Dantès. At the end of this section, however, the story is propelled via a long, intricate monologue delivered by Bertuccio. In it, he explains his connection to many of the main characters, particularly his history with Villefort and Caderousse. Nothing Bertuccio has to say is revelatory. All the details he thinks he is exposing are details that the Count already knows. But the expository monologue is a sign of Dumas's love for storytelling through his words of his characters as well as their actions. In other words, he writes like a dramatist.

The surprise arrival of Maximilian Morrel at Albert's breakfast party feels incongruous at first, but it soon becomes apparent that he is there to add dimension to the character of the Count, who, upon seeing him, feels positive emotions that he thought he had lost forever. The sight of Maximilian is heartwarming in this context, underlining the effect the Morrel family has on the Count. His presence also foreshadows future events with which the Count will have to deal, again involving the Morrels.

Finally, the portrait of Mercédès is a tie to the Count's former life and former humanity. She is drawn looking at the sea, almost forlornly, suggesting that she is still waiting for her sailor, Dantès, to come back to her so that they can start a life together. Her costume, too, is a strong, visual reminder of better days. She has not forgotten or abandoned him, and her connection to him remains as strong as the day they met. (The portrait's symbolism is not lost on Fernand, either, who despises it and had it removed from their home.) The undying power of her love for him is also illustrated in her immediate recognition of the Count as Dantès. She alone knows him the best, and she alone is effortlessly able to see through his facade.

Chapters 47-53

Chapter 47: Unlimited Credit

The Count of Monte Cristo is now ready to draw the families of his enemies, Danglars and Villefort, into his web of revenge. First, he orders Bertuccio to buy Danglars's two most splendid horses for double the price of what is stated. He also knows that the animals technically are the property of Madame Danglars. Upon their acquisition, the Count harnesses them to his personal coach and rides over to Danglars's home. As the title suggests, he requests the opening of an unlimited line of credit with him. Danglars is both shocked and grateful.

Chapter 48: The Dapper Grays

As the Count waits at the Danglars home, Madame Danglars arrives and goes haywire when she sees her horses attached to his coach. She becomes furious with her husband for selling them. The Count departs from the scene, as does Lucien Debray, her clandestine lover.

Later that same day, the Count gives the horse back in a feigned act of kindness. He is also aware of the fact that Madame d'Villefort is scheduled to borrow the horse the following day. Therefore, he arranges for the horses to be released, strategically when they approach his home. Madame d'Villefort is consumed with fear, with her son, Edward, panicking as well. Ali, the Count's servant, easily lassos them, saving the Villeforts from harm. It is too late for Edward however, who faints from his fears. The Count revives him using a mysterious potion.

Chapter 49: Ideology

Villefort pays the Count a visit in gratitude for saving his family from the horses. Having the opportunity, the Count begins a discussion with Villefort on justice, specifically, natural justice versus legal. In the course of the conversation, Villefort reveals that his father has suffered a paralyzing stroke.

Chapter 50: Haydée

The Count visits Haydée, his gorgeous slave. She has her own living quarters, which are decorated in an Asian-inspired opulence. He wants her to know that whatever she chooses to do – stay with him or leave to pursue her own life – is completely up to her, and he will approve regardless. She tells the Count that her loyalty to him is unwavering, but he retorts by reminding her that she is still merely a child. The future may bring a different mindset. Still, she has his full support in any decision. The only condition he has is that she never reveals the circumstances of her mysterious birth to anyone.

Chapter 51: The Morrel Family

The Count visits Maximilian Morrel, who is staying with Julie, his sister, who has married Emmanuel Herbaut, the young clerk in the employ of her father and the couple for whom the Count made marriage possible. He is taken aback by their home's utter tranquility, happiness, and above all else, love. He makes a comment about this very thing, and the couple answers by telling him the story of the red purse and the diamond. They also tell the Count how very much they wish they could know the identity of the person who was so instrumental in their happiness. He offers them a theory that it might have been Lord Wilmore, an Englishman rumored to perform such acts of kindness and generosity. Maximilian, however, shares his father's belief that it was Edmund Dantès, acting as an angel. The Count is overcome with emotion by these statements and leaves before giving himself away.

Chapter 52: Pyramus and Thisbe

Maximilian goes to the Villefort home and waits at the gate of the garden, where he secretly meets the love of his life, Valentine d'Villefort, Villefort's daughter from his first marriage. Valentine pours her heart of to Maximilian about her unfortunate lot in life: her father ignores her, and she is hated by her stepmother. To make matters even worse, she is engaged to a man she doesn't love, Franz d'Epinay. Maximilian tells her that she must promise herself that the marriage will not take place, no matter how strongly her parents promote it. Like Romeo and Juliet, the two lovers discuss the obstacles they face – Maximilian hasn't the money or position to support a wife of Valentine's social class, and even more, her father has a long standing hatred for the Morrel family. As they commiserate, the Count of Monte Cristo arrives at the Villefort's home. Valentine is called away.

Chapter 53: Toxicology

The Count tells Madame d'Villefort that they were previously introduced in Italy. She remembers the encounter, including the detail that while in Italy, the Count of Monte Cristo was respected as a noble doctor, having saved the lives of two people. She begins to inquire about his background in chemistry, and more specifically, toxic substances. He explains the procedure he designed to build up his poison, adding that he also has a very effective "antispasmodic" substance in his possession. In fact, it is the same substance he used to revive Edward when he fainted from fear over the wild horses. In small doses, it is incredibly useful and safe; however, in larger ones, it is fatal. What intrigues Madame d'Villefort the most is that the drug kills in a seemingly innocent way – the victim appears to perish from natural causes, thus shifting focus away from the potion. The Count understands Madame d'Villefort's subtle message, so to speak, and extends an offer to send her some of it the following day.

Analysis: Chapters 47 through 53

Dumas reintroduces Villefort in this section to represent what he sees as some of the ills of his society, specifically, what is inherently wrong with the judicial system. Villefort is portrayed as strict and unyielding, promoting the kind of justice that the Count sees as ineffective and even irrelevant. Caring not at all for the humanistic side of justice, Villefort is consumed with the letter of the law, prosecution and punishment. He has no time or interest in anything life-enhancing or cultured, such as art or music, and is driven only by the ability to impose the rigidity of the law on others. For Dumas, this posture reflects the same scenario that exists in society at large: how the judicial system basically lacks human compassion, and is especially hard on those living in more difficult financial circumstances. Coupled with his, and society's lack of compassion is Villefort's own hypocrisy. Again, just like the hypocrisy that exists in society, Villefort has no remorse when he himself breaks the law, such as sending Dantes to prison unjustifiably, or when he tries to end the life of his own illegitimate infant son. Like the society in which he navigates, Villefort's lack of ethics and morality go unpunished because he enjoys a higher social position. According to the Count, modern societies are unfair and unduly oppressive towards less wealthy citizens, and do not only not protect all citizens but instead, persecute the less fortunate.

In contrast to the inflexible, strict and self-interested characters such as Villefort, Dumas presents the reader with more details about Haydée. She is an archetype of the Romantic posture – sensual, loving, exotic, indulgent and emotionally charged. Her influence on the Count makes him even more alluring and mysterious, and his infatuation with Middle Eastern and Asian-inspired design, food, décor, etc., is, in part, due to his connection to her. They are, quite simply, exotic, and not in line with Western European tradition.

Although the Count's exoticism is *sympatico* with Haydée's, that is where the similarity ends. Dumas gives the reader several instances in this section where his behavior, or more precisely, his skewed mental outlook, is shown. Consumed with revenge, he has become so out of touch with positive human emotions that any hint of experiencing them throws him off balance. Where most people welcome happiness, he actively rejects it, and takes a ritualistic approach to preparing himself for avoiding it at all costs. Still, his visit to the Morrel home compromises his stoic stance – this is the only family he knows which truly loves unconditionally, which is appreciative of kindness, and which recognizes real generosity. When he is confronted by these virtuous tendencies, he must bolt away, as he no longer has the resources to deal with goodness. They go against his bleak and negative opinion of mankind in general, which, sadly, is often realized through and supported by the bad actions of those around him; however, the Morrels are the only exception to this rule, and their generosity of spirit is something that is, tragically, no longer on his radar.

Chapters 54-62

Chapter 54: Robert Le Diable

The tongues of the gossips wag as the Count and Haydée attend the opera. He meanders over to the box of Madame Danglars, where Eugénie, Albert, and Fernand are also sitting. As the Count speaks with Fernand, Haydée sees something that gravely upsets her. The Count excuses himself and returns to her, only to find her overcome. She tells the Count that she has seen the man who turned on her father, Ali Pacha, and sold her into slavery. That man, it turns out, is Fernand.

Chapter 55: A Talk about Stocks

Albert de Morcerf and Lucien Debray visit the Count, and the men chat about Albert's recent engagement to Eugénie Danglars, the Danglars's young, beautiful daughter. Albert is not at all excited about the arrangement, as although she is quite lovely, he finds her overly intelligent and somewhat masculine. In addition, Mercédès, his mother, is not fond of the Danglars family, and does not want the tie to them that comes with marriage. Albert, a good son, does not want to upset his mother.

The men then start to discuss Madame Danglars. Debray mentions that she s known to gamble away lots of her husband's money playing the stock market. Albert makes a joke about it, saying that she should be taught a lesson through false reportage, to which Debray reacts nervously. The Count realizes that Debray has been breaking the law by giving his lover insider trading information.

Chapter 56: Major Cavalcanti

The Count meets with two men and promises them a hefty sum for pretending to be people they are not. The older man is to be Marquis Bartolomeo Cavalcanti, a retired Italian major who, for fifteen years, has been unsuccessfully searching for his kidnapped son.

Chapter 57: Andrea Cavalcanti

The younger man is instructed to play Bartolomeo Cavalcanti's son, Andrea Cavalcanti, who has been reunited with his father through the intervention of the Count. The Count gives them everything they need for authenticity – clothing, documents, and more. He then tells them they must attend a party – in full "character" – that he is giving in a few days.

Chapter 58: At the Gate

Maximilian and Valentine meet again at Valentine's family garden. He tells her that Franz will be coming back to Paris. What will they do? Valentine says that she cannot go against her father's wishes. She also adds that her stepmother has been promoting convent life. (She wants her son Edward to be the sole heir of the Villefort estate.) They then discuss the fated engagement of Albert and Eugénie, neither of whom wants to marry the other. Instead, Eugénie has told Valentine that she wants to live the life of an independent, bohemian, unmarried artist.

Chapter 59: M. Noirtier d'Villefort

Villefort and his wife visit Noirtier's room, where he lives with his servant, Barrois, in a section of their house. The stroke has left the elder man incapable of communicating, except with Villefort, Barrois, and Valentine. Valentine is the apple of her grandfather's eye, and as such, she can read his thoughts. Villefort and his wife tell Noirtier about Valentine's engagement. This agitates him, as Franz's father has always been his adversary. Valentine is called to calm her grandfather down, and while doing so, confesses that she does not want to go through with the marriage. He makes a promise to help her get out of the arrangement.

Chapter 60: The Will

In line with his plan to help Valentine, Noirtier changes the terms of his will to state that if she marries Franz, her entire inheritance will go to charity. Villefort still will not acquiesce. He refuses to cancel the engagement.

Chapter 61: The Telegraph

The Count Monte Cristo waits for the Villeforts downstairs in order to invite them to his party. He also asks them advice on a good telegraph office. They suggest the Spanish line.

Chapter 62: The Bribe

The Count arrives at a remote telegraph officer, where he pays the employee to create a false telegraph. Debray hurries to the Danglars household to tell his lover that he has just learned from confidential government sources (or perhaps a mysterious telegraph…) that a revolution in Spain is imminent. She must therefore sell all of her husband's Spanish bonds. She does, but it is soon reported that no such revolution is taking place. Danglars winds up losing one million francs.

Analysis: Chapters 54 through 62

It is easy to see why *The Count of Monte Cristo* is often categorized as a melodrama. Actions are mysterious and over-the-top, with an unusual main character who can accomplish outlandish, almost impossible feats. Still, to pigeonhole the novel is to do it a disservice, as for all of the melodrama, Dumas also makes a point of peppering the book with social commentary and even satire. At the onset of this section, the reader sees a night at the opera much like any night among the upper classes of the times would be, complete with private boxes and male chaperones for the women in attendance. But the author has a way of bumping these realistic events up a notch into the sphere of satire when, for example, he makes the point of the fact that, for all their traditions and rules of etiquette, it was perfectly acceptable among this class to have one's lover be your attending chaperone (in this case, Debray and Madame Danglars). In this one small detail, he skewers the hypocrisy of the so-called aristocracy.

In this section, Noirtier is also reintroduced to the reader, drawn in a way to evoke sympathy and allegiance. This is a bit of a switch, as the character had been depicted as a man whose commitment to ideas far exceeded his commitment to other people. Still, the ideas to which he subscribed were, for Dumas, noble at the core, and the fact that Noirtier was always at odds with Villefort certainly makes him worthy of admiration.

Finally, the Count's planned downfall of Danglars is evident in this section of the book, via the intricate plan involving the false telegraph. The Count attacks Danglars on the thing he treasures the most – his money – and his slow and steady descent into financial ruin are carefully orchestrated for the fullest impact. Other elements of the plan are much more subtle, as the book's progression will reveal, but are nonetheless the handiwork of the Count.

Chapters 63-67

Chapter 63: Shadows

The night of the Count's dinner party has finally arrived. His new home in Auteuil looks spectacular, complete with exciting renovations. But two areas have been left untouched: the garden, and a minor-sized bedroom. Maximilian Morrel is the first to arrive; next, the Danglars and their "friend," Lucien Debray.

The Count proceeds to introduce his special guests, "Major Bartolomeo Cavalcanti" and his son, "Andrea," the hired con men. Just as the Count had expected, Danglars is extremely taken with the idea of an extravagantly wealthy nobleman at the affair, especially after hearing that Andrea is seeking a wife while in Paris. Before long, the Villeforts arrive. When Bertuccio sees Madame Danglars among the partygoers, he is stunned. He shares with the Count that she is the same woman who used to secretly meet Villefort in this house. Bertuccio's surprise is compounded when he sees Villefort, as he thought he had killed him years ago. The Count tells Bertuccio that the stabbing that ensued only injured Villefort; it was not fatal, as Bertuccio had believed. If all this were not enough, Bertuccio's night of surprises is not over: when he sees the appealing "Andrea Cavalcanti," he recognizes him as his rogue son, Benedetto.

Chapter 64: The Dinner

After dinner, the Count puts into motion a means to taunt some of his guests. He brings everyone to the unchanged bedroom, and begins to share a theory that he has about it being the site of a violent crime. He cannot prove it, but he senses it strongly. He gets even more specific by telling them that he thinks a newborn baby was killed – smothered to death – in the room. Then he takes the guests to the garden, and shows them a spot where he found the skeletal remains of a baby. As his theory unravels, so do Madame Danglars and Villefort. As the Count casually invites everyone for an after-dinner coffer, the two guilty parties plan to meet the next day.

Chapter 65: The Beggar

As Benedetto climbs into his carriage to leave the party, he is stopped by Caderousse, who has escaped from prison. The two man have a common criminal history. He demands that his old friend Benedetto give him 200 francs a month or he will blow his cover. Benedetto, fearing that he'll be found out, agrees.

Chapter 66: A Conjugal Scene

Now home, Madame Danglars goes to bed, accompanied by Debray. Danglars bursts into the room and asks Debray to leave him and his wife alone, shocking the lovers with this unprecedented request. With Debray gone, he confronts Madame with the financial scenario that has been taking place, namely, Debray's trading information that has, up until now, made Danglars a lot of money. Basically he tells his wife that he has overlooked their martial arrangement, and even her participation in the market's illegal activities, but this extreme loss of money is too much to bear. Moreover, he resents the fact that Debray has not offered to offset Danglers's losses, as he was, in Danglars's eyes, responsible for them. Finally, he brings up her numerous dalliances over the years, and ultimately reveals that he knows all about the child she bore with Villefort and how it drove her first husband to suicide.

Chapter 67: Matrimonial Plans

The day after the party, Danglars visits the Count to find out more about Andrea Cavalcanti. Knowing that Andrea wants to marry, he mentions that he thinks his own daughter would be the perfect mate, and that her current beau, Albert, is neither a real nobleman or of the appropriate social standing. Albert is actually the son of a poor fisherman named Fernand Mondego. The Count, of course, already knows all these details, but hides that from Danglars. He mentions that he has heard of a man named Fernand, and that he was accused of betraying Ali Pasha, Haydée's father, to the Turks. He suggests that Danglars to contact his network in Yanina to reveal the truth about Fernand and his role in Ali's betrayal.

Analysis: Chapters 63 through 67

Dumas once again indulges his contemporary reader's Romantic preoccupation with the eerie and grotesque by having the Count go on about his theoretical murder mystery involving forbidden love and the death of a baby. Gothic romances were quite the rage in Dumas's day, and surely had an influence on his own writing. Dumas also showcases the terror experienced by Madame Danglars and Villefort upon hearing the Count convey their past step by step, culminating with the death of a baby. The Count is so cold-blooded in his approach that it almost makes them the underdogs against such a strong, dominant force of revenge. For this reason, *The Count of Monte Cristo* can certainly rank as a gothic novel.

Speaking of revenge, it takes the front seat yet again in this section as both Bertuccio and Haydée see people they never expected to see (Villefort and Fernand, respectively), and hope for revenge on these same figures. A solitary figure, the Count delights in the fact that his enemies are also the enemies of the two people closest to him. They can share their desire to avenge the wrongdoings done to them, and since revenge is the only motivator in the Count's life at present, it draws him even closer.

Chapters 68-76

Chapter 68: The Office of the Procureur du Roi

Madame Danglars visits Villefort's office. The two are completely thrown by the fact that the Count might know their secrets. Still, Villefort is convinced that the Count is bluffing. He couldn't possibly have found the infant's skeleton, as the body was never buried. Bertuccio stole the box with the baby inside after thinking he had stabbed Villefort to death. Villefort deduces that the baby must have survived; otherwise, it only makes sense that Bertuccio would have contacted the authorities about the baby's death, and had he believed Villefort was dead. But the fact remains that Villefort and Madame Danglars are in trouble, as the Count is nipping at their heels. Villefort makes a vow that he will find out who the Count really is, and what is behind his agenda.

Chapter 69: A Summer Ball

Albert goes to visit the Count. He invites him to a gala his family is holding.

Chapter 70: The Inquiry

Villefort tries to uncover the Count's identity by contacting some of his well-placed friends. He finds out that there are two former friends of the Count currently living in Paris: one, an Italian priest called Abbé Busoni, and another, an English nobleman known as Lord Wilmore. Villefort requests that the police commissioner visit the priest first. Busoni, who is actually the Count, tells the commissioner that he has known the Count for years, and shares that the mysteries count is the son of a wealthy shipbuilder from Malta. In a strange twist, he also tells the commissioner that Lord Wilmore is a long time enemy of the Count.

Villefort visits Wilmore (the Count in disguise yet again), who states that the Count made his fortune via a Middle Eastern silver mine. Villefort specifically asks why the Count bought his home in Auteuil. Lord Wilmore's answer is that the Count wants to cultivate a mineral spring on the property. Villefort is happy to hear this development.

Chapter 71: The Ball

At the Morcerfs' gala, the Count captivates all the guests; however, Mercédès observes that he takes nothing in the way of food or drink all night.

Chapter 72: Bread and Salt

Mercédès coaxes the Count away from the gala and brings him to the garden. Once there, she encourages him to eat some fruit, which he refuses. She is insulted, as it is an Arabian custom that people who share food together are forever friends. They then dance around the details of their past without ever really admitting that they know each other. Suddenly, Villefort appears. He is looking for his wife and daughter, as he has news that the Marquis de Saint Méran, the father of his former wife, has died.

Chapter 73: Madame de Saint-Méran

On the same night her husband dies, Madame de Saint-Méran takes ill. She senses that she will die in the morning. She is also distraught from seeing someone in white tampering with the glass that rests by her bedside. Knowing that she only has a short time to live, she is even more determined to see her granddaughter Valentine married to Franz. Of course, Valentine does not want to, as she is in love with Maximilian, but she knows that Madame would not approve given his financial status.

Chapter 74: The Promise

Maximilian and Valentine meet at the garden at the Villefort home. He tells her that Franz has returned, and is ready to get married, and therefore begs Valentine to run away with him. She agrees.

Later, Maximilian is waiting to meet Valentine as planned, but she never arrives. Panicked, he goes to the Villefort home to see if he can solve the mystery of her absence.
While there, he overhears Villefort and a doctor discussing the death of Madame de Saint-Méran, which the doctor believes is a murder by a poison called brucine, which Noirtier has been taking in safe doses for health purposes. Now even more scared, Maximilian sneaks into the house and finds Valentine. She introduces him to her grandfather, Noirtier, who shares with the young couple his intentions to prevent Valentine from marrying Franz.

Chapter 75: The Villefort Family Vault

The marquis and marquise are buried, and Franz d'Epinay soon arrives at the Villeforts to formalize his contract of marriage to Valentine; however, before they put pen to paper, Barrois interrupts with the news that Noirtier wants to speak with Franz.

Chapter 76: A Signed Statement

Noirtier tells Barrois to retrieve papers from his desk and give them to Franz. The papers prove that Noirtier killed Franz's father in a duel. Villefort, mortified and shocked, runs from the scene.

Analysis: Chapters 68 through 76

It's no wonder that *The Count of Monte Cristo* has been a favorite with filmmakers, as the character of the Count is a culmination of mystery, intrigue, strength, intelligence and action. One can never be sure where he will show up next, and in what kind of persona. In fact, his ability to disguise his real identity is so skilled that even those closest to him are left wondering. He is one of literature's premier Masters of Disguise, adding to his incredible appeal.

The Count also has a bit of the sleuth in him – a Romantic Sherlock Holmes, one might say. He is obsessed with the acquisition of facts and details so that he can appropriately execute his mission(s). He also knows quite well how to push people's buttons in order for them to be putty in his hands. Clever and somewhat manipulative, the Count has an established set of goals that he is determined to meet: he wants to bring justice to those who deserve it and punish those at fault for criminal and/or immoral activity. However, he will not stoop to criminal activity himself to do so, but rather, chooses to expose the sins of his nemeses and let the rest unfold accordingly. In more colloquial terms, give them enough rope to hang themselves.

These chapters reveal an interesting connection between Noirtier and Franz d'Epinay's father. They are long term enemies, which places Villefort in a more precarious place than ever. He certainly knows about the murder committed, as he references it earlier in the novel when he tells his father that he is wanted by the authorities. And the imminent marriage between his daughter and Franz will, ultimately, ensure that Noirtier's crime will never be revealed due to family connections, saving his own reputation in the process. But by now, it is no surprise to anyone that Villefort's actions are solely motivated by self-interest, even if it means his daughter is destined for a loveless marriage and miserable life.

Chapters 77-84

Chapter 77: Progress of M. Cavalcanti the Younger

The Count and "Andrea Cavalcanti" go to visit Danglars. Eugénie leaves the festivities to play music with her teacher, Louise d'Armilly, to whom she has grown quite close. Danglars wants Andrea included in the musical merriment, as he has designs on him for a son-in-law. Albert arrives soon after, but Danglars shows him nothing but contempt.

Chapter 78: Haydée

On their journey back to the Count's residence, Albert makes light of Danglars's less than subtle agenda regarding Andrea. He then asks the Count if he could meet Haydée, and the Count agrees under one condition: Albert must not reveal the identity of his father. Haydée shares the story of her father, Ali Pacha, with Albert, telling him that he ruled over Yanina, a Greek state. During this time, his closest assistant was a French-born soldier. The solider betrayed Ali by surrendering his castle to the Turks, propelling Ali's eventual murder. He then sold Ali's wife and daughter (Haydée) into slavery. Her mother soon died, but Haydée was thankfully rescued by the Count who bought her freedom. The whole series of events makes Albert dizzy, and he listens, having no idea that the Frenchman about whom she speaks is actually his father.

Chapter 79: Yanina

Franz sends a nasty correspondence to Villefort, backing out of his engagement to Valentine. Noirtier changes his will, bequeathing his entire estate to Valentine provided that they are never separated. Meanwhile, Fernand goes to see Danglars to discuss the engagement of their children, Albert and Eugénie. Danglars tells him that the engagement off, and gives no excuse or reason for the change of heart.

Out of the blue, Beauchamp's newspaper reveals a story stating that a man by the name of Fernand was behind orchestrating Ali Pacha's capture and death by the Turks. It never names the Count de Morcef specifically; however, Albert takes the article as slander against his father. The Count tries to calm the young man down, but Albert gives Beauchamp and ultimatum: either retract the story or the two men will duel. Beauchamp requests a three week stay in order to do some fact-finding about the story before resorting to anything more drastic like a duel.

Chapter 80: The Lemonade

Barrois goes to get Maximilian per the request of Noirtier. As Albert, Noirtier, and Valentine discuss plans for the future, a thirsty Barrois reaches over and takes a sip of Noirtier's glass of lemonade. Ina matter of moments, he is dead. The doctor who is called tells them that brucine is in the lemonade. Noirtier has also ingested some of the lemonade, but was not affected. The fact that he takes brucine regularly in smaller doses since his strokes has built up a tolerance to it.

Chapter 81: The Accusation

The doctor is certain that the poison was meant for Noirtier, and suspects that Valentine is behind the scheme given her status as sole heiress to Noirtier's fortune.

Chapter 82: The Room of the Retired Baker

Caderousse tells Benedetto that the 200 francs a month he has been receiving to keep

Benedetto's secret is not enough. He wants an increase. Benedetto tells Caderousse that he thinks that the Count is his biological father. If so, he is in line for a substantial fortune upon the Count's death. To investigate this theory, Caderousse decides to break into the Count's home in Paris while the Count is away at Auteuil.

Chapter 83: The Burglary

The following day, the Count receives an unsigned warning that his house is going to be burglarized. He tells his entire staff to leave the premises, with only him and Ali remaining. The two men, both armed, wait for the burglar, who breaks a bedroom window as his entryway. But Ali spies a second figure on the property, waiting outside.

As the Count observes the burglar trying to break into his desk, he recognizes him as Caderousse. He quickly dons the garments of "Abbé Busoni," and confronts the thief, who is now stricken with fear. Abbé Busoni offers Caderousse his freedom on the condition that he tells him 1/ how he escaped from prison, and 2/ why he is burglarizing the Count's home. Caderousse confesses that an Englishman named Lord Wilmore sent Benedetto a sharp file while incarcerated. Benedetto and Caderousse were shackled together, so both men were able to file away the chains. He also tells the priest that he is now in criminal cahoots with Benedetto, with Benedetto paying him for his silence. Abbé Busoni pretends to be shocked by the news that Andrea Cavalcanti, who is now the fiancé of Eugénie Danglars, has a criminal past and is now a deceptive phony. He tells Caderousse that Benedetto must be exposed. This sets Caderousse into a fit, and he tries to kill Busoni with a dagger; however, Busoni is protected by a chain-mail garment under his robes, preventing injury. Busoni then forces Caderousse to compose a letter to Danglars, exposing Benedetto's true identity, after which he allows him to leave through the broken window. He tells Caderousse that his safe return home will be a sign from God, symbolizing His forgiveness for Caderousse's actions. This is all a ruse, as the Count/Busoni is aware that Benedetto is the figure in waiting seen earlier by Ali, and that he will likely murder Caderousse.

Chapter 84: The Hand of God

Once outside, Benedetto stabs Caderousse. The Count brings Caderousse into his home. He makes the injured man sign a statement revealing that Benedetto was his murderer. As he nears death, the Count chastises Caserousse for his immoral actions, and tells him to seek God's mercy before he dies. Caderousse refuses, at which point the Count shares his true identity, Edmond Dantès. Upon the news, Caderousse, overwhelmed, acknowledges that a higher presence must surely exist. He then dies. The police initiate a manhunt for Benedetto.

Analysis: Chapters 77 through 84

Although he did not kill him himself, Caderousse's death is the first time the reader sees an actual event that the Count has orchestrated in order to achieve justice, and in fact sets the wheels in motion for the demise of his remaining enemies. All the details are in place: Danglars's fortune dwindles by the minute, and his daughter is now engaged to Benedetto, a criminal; moreover, murderers are obviously lurking about Villefort's home, and the son he thought he killed years ago is navigating the social circle of Paris. The Count can now sit back and watches the pieces fall.

As he comes closer to his death, the character of Caderousse is further examined. For almost his entire life, Caderousse has been a miserable, unhappy and dissatisfied man, exemplifying a tenet that Dumas supports: that happiness comes from within, not from acquisitions or even other people. (He illustrates this earlier in the novel by depicting the simple, loving happiness that exists in the home of Julie and Emmanuel Herbaut.) As Caderousse lies dying, he and the Count reflect on all the wrongdoings Caderousse has been responsible for, and how they have been motivated by greed and avarice. Nothing was ever enough, even the fortune Abbé Busoni had surprisingly provided, or the fact that he managed to escape a life in prison, or even the money he bribed out of Benedetto. He repeatedly took the criminal road to satisfy his greed, but only really secured his misery. His posture is in direct contrast to that of the Herbauts.

Caderousse's last minutes also illustrate an unusual contrast as he and Abbé Busoni discuss the dying man's unfortunate life choices. Instead of offering forgiveness and redemption at a time of death, which is what an actual Catholic priest would do, Abbé Busoni condemns him. This places the Count/Abbé Busoni in conflict with the Christian doctrine of mercy. Still, the author continually surrounds the Count with Christian language and imagery, such as Dantès' "baptism" when escaping prison, and even the title of Count of Monte Cristo, which translates into mountain of Christ. Romantic writers were often preoccupied with the potential for reconciliation between religious traditions and individual freedoms, and Dumas shared this interest.

Chapters 85-88

Chapter 85: Beauchamp

After continuing his investigation which took him to Yanina, Beauchamp shares his findings with Albert. He has proof positive that the accusations against Morcerf are, in fact, valid. But because the men are friends, Beauchamp assures Albert that he will keep the information about his father under wraps. Albert is completely stunned and depressed, but thanks Beauchamp for his cooperation and understanding.

Chapter 86: The Journey

Albert is invited by the Count to accompany him on a trip to Normandy, where the Count has another residence. After three days of relaxation, Albert receives notice from Beauchamp that he must return to Paris immediately. Beauchamp has also included an article from a competitive newspaper which details Morcerf's involvement in the Ali Pacha case. This eliminates any shadow of doubt regarding Morcerf's guilt.

Chapter 87: The Trial

Upon his return, Albert goes to Beauchamp's home asking for details. Beauchamp tells him that a gentleman from Yanina arrived in Paris armed with documents which point to Morcerf's guilt, thus providing the basis for the article which appeared in the other newspaper. Even worse, because Morcerf is a member of the Chamber, a trial was arranged immediately.

Beauchamp tells Albert that Haydée testified against Morcerf, telling the court that he was the man who betrayed her father, helped his enemies murder him and steal his fortune, and then sold her and her mother into slavery. She even has a document stating that her freedom was bought by the Count of Monte Cristo from a man named Fernand Mondego, and that the man had a noticeable scar on his hand that matched the scar on Morcerf's. Morcerf was found guilty as charged.

Chapter 88: The Challenge

Albert tells Beauchamp that he will do everything in his power to revenge his father's embarrassment and downfall. He will even kill the man responsible for it. Beauchamp tells him to be reasonable, but it falls on deaf ears. He tells Albert that he will help him find the man, and then adds that Danglars has been in Yanina of late, asking people what they knew about Morcerf. Albert arrives at Danglars's home where he finds him with Andrea. He challenges them both to a duel. Danglars tells Albert that the Count was the one who suggested that he make inquiries at Yanina. Albert figures out that, since the Count knows all Haydée's past, that he must have already known the truth about his father. He then decides to challenge the Count to a duel for honor's sake.

Analysis: Chapters 85 through 88

The news about his father's past has put Albert into a state of panic and revenge. He is out for blood: he wants to act, and act violently, and it is anyone's guess as to what he will do next in the name of vengeance. He has even been a threat to Beauchamp, his friend, simply because the newspaperman was indirectly involved in exposing the story. More irrational, he challenges Andrea, who has had absolutely no role in the entire affair.

Albert's reaction runs parallel to the theme of the individual's fight against fate. Albert wants to be proactive and not simply be a passive bystander as things unravel. He wants some kind of control, albeit and irrational kind. This trait of attempting to fight fate links Albert to the Count, who also plays by his own rules.

Dumas does not yet reveal, however, the Count's true feelings about Albert, or whether or not he resents him solely for his connection to Morcerf, his enemy. When the men first meet, it is clear that the Count is repulsed for some reason; however, as the novel continues, the Count begins to grow fond of the young man, especially when he displays kindnesses such as his loyalty to his mother, Mercédès. The Count must acknowledge that Albert is not Fernand, but is a better man.

As Fernand's ruin becomes more apparent, the Count begins to sympathize with Albert, recognizing the young man's pain and suffering. His invitation to Normandy may hold a clue to his feelings: did the Count bring Albert there to save him from seeing his father's downfall, or did he take him away so that Morcerf would be denied of his son's support in a time of crisis and despair?

Chapters 89-93

Chapter 89: The Insult

Albert and Beauchamp rush to the Count's residence, but are told that he is not greeting any guests at this time. The servant does, however, tell them that his master plans to go to the opera that night. Albert tells Franz, Debray, and Maximilian to meet him at the opera house that night as well. Next, he visits his mother and asks her if she knows why the Count holds such contempt for Morcerf. Mercédès tries to quell Albert's anger, asking him to remember that the Count was his friend.

After Albert leaves, Mercédès dispatches one of her servants to trail Albert that night. At the opera house, Albert forcefully enters the Count's box and challenges him to a duel. The duel will take place at 8:00AM the next morning, using pistols. The Count requests that Maximilian and Emmanuel accompany him to the duel as his assistants.

Chapter 90: Mercédès

A desperate Mercédès visits the Count, who explains to her the reasons behind his contempt for Fernand. He produces the false documents against Dantès that were forwarded to the authorities those many years ago (and sealing his fate of imprisonment). Mercédès is overcome with grief, and asks for his forgiveness as she states that she never stopped loving

Edmond Dantès. She then begs the Count to somehow spare her son's life, as he is not the guilty party – her husband is. The Count cannot refuse his former love's requests, and tells her that Albert will not be harmed. Still, for honor's sake, he must fight the duel, implying that he will sacrifice his own life to save Albert's.

Chapter 91: The Meeting

Monte Cristo share his plan to allow his own death with Maximilian and Emmanuel. He then affirms his unparalleled skill with the weapon so that they known his death was intentional. Albert arrives at the duel's designated site, but surprisingly reneges. Instead, he offers the Count an apology for his wrongful accusations. The Count deduces that the young man's mother has filled him in on their prior conversation, exposing Morcerf for the man he is.

Chapter 92: The Mother and Son

Albert and Mercédès make plans to leave the area and start a new life without the encumbrances of Fernand's reputation. As they are getting ready to go, she receives a letter from the Count, telling her to go to the former home of Louis Dantès in Marseilles. In the front of the house, she will find a tree on the lawn, under which she can access a small amount of money that Edmond had buried there years ago when he dreamed of starting a life with Mercédès. It should be enough for her to support herself. Touched, she accepts his gift, and tells him that she will use it to enter her new life in a nunnery.

Chapter 93: The Suicide

The Count arrives home to find Haydée waiting for him. It occurs to him that he might be falling in love with her. They are enjoying the moment when Fernand interrupts, furious that Albert reneged on the duel. Fernand then challenges the Count to a duel of his own, but before it happens, he tells the Count that he must know his true identity. The Count leaves the room, only to return in the clothing of a sailor. The image allows Fernand to immediately recognize him as Edmond Dantès. Struck with utter fear and panic, he runs from the house. At his own home, he finds that his family is deserting him. As his wife and son leave, he shoots himself.

Analysis: Chapters 89 through 93

In this section, the reader learns that the Mercédès of today is fundamentally the same person she was when she was in love with Dantès so many years ago. When Mercédès first goes to the Count to plea for her son's life, he is skeptical; however, she proves her mettle in his eyes by telling her son the story of his father's crimes against Dantès, even if it means irrevocably discrediting Fernand's name to Albert. Another woman might allow the Count to sacrifice himself in order to save her son; however, Mercédès takes the high road and tries to be fair to all parties involved. Her gracious act saves both her son and the Count. Many scholars view Mercédès as the novel's moral compass: she is both decent and intelligent, and her actions reflect this. Not only is she the only person in the Count circle who immediately recognizes him, but she is also honorable enough to not want the Count to die in order to save her son. She also has a component of forgiveness to her character, which is a scarce trait in the novel's environment. Finally, she chooses to forfeit her comfortable lifestyle for life in a convent, as she cannot reconcile the evil acts which led to her family's social position. Mercédès is perhaps the only character thus far whose innate goodness can crack the Count's facade.

Shakespeare's Juliet asked, "What's in a name?" This question has relevance here as well. When Mercédès and the Count of Monte Cristo first meet after all those years apart, she calls him Edmond, and asks him to, in turn, call her Mercédès and not Madame de Morcerf. This act is a throwback to the past, and signifies that the simplicity of those people – Edmond and Mercédès - represents all that is good and decent. Their names separate them from the aristocratic trappings that they are now enmeshed in.

Chapters 94-102

Chapter 94: Valentine

Maximilian goes to visit his love, Valentine. He finds her feeling ill, and when she drinks, everything has a bitter taste.

Madame Danglers and Eugénie pay Valentine a visit as well. They share the news that Eugénie will imminently be marrying Andrea Cavalcanti, much to Eugénie's chagrin. She is not interested in marriage, but instead would rather pursue her life as an independent artist.

Valentine returns to Maximilian and Noirtier. Her illness has escalated, and she passes out.

Chapter 95: The Confession

Maximilian goes to the Count, pleading for assistance. Initially, the Count appears aloof; however, when he realizes how much Maximilian loves Valentine, he pledges his help to save her life.

At the Villefort home, the doctor who has been summoned confides in Noirtier, who is savvy to the latest turn of events, what could be going on. The old man knows that his granddaughter has been poisoned. He actually suspected that she would be the next target, so therefore has been building up her immunity to brucine by giving her small regular doses.

In the midst of this chaos, "Abbé Busoni" rents the house next to the Villeforts.

Chapter 96: The Father and Daughter

Eugénie tells her father that she refuses to marry Andrea Cavalcanti, but he responds with the fact that his finances are in ruin, and that the only thing that will save him is her marriage to Andrea. He continues by saying that Andrea's money will allow him the wiggle room he needs to revitalize his credit and invest in the American railroad system.

Eugénie agrees to the marriage provided that Danglars only uses the promise of Andrea's money as the basis for his loan.

Chapter 97: The Contract

The marriage contract between Andrea and Eugénie goes on as planned, and Danglars throws a party to celebrate. As the contract itself is about to be signed, the Count tells the crowd about the letter Caderousse wrote to Danglars, and states that the letter was confiscated from Caderousse's clothing and given to Villefort. He neglects to mention what the letter conveys, but before long, two officers of the law appear, looking as if they are there to arrest Andrea, who has mysteriously and craftily disappeared.

Chapter 98: The Departure for Belgium

Eugénie is miserable. As her engagement party guest begin to leave, she flees to her room with her companion and teacher, Louise d'Armilly, and they begin to talk about how they want to escape together to Italy via Belgium that very night to pursue their music. Eugénie intends to disguise herself as a man, acting as brother to Louise. She is determined to see their plan through, and cuts off all her hair. After dressing in men's attire and packing up their belongings, the two women set out in a carriage.

Chapter 99: The Hotel of the Bell and the Bottle

Parallel to Eugénie's plan to escape Paris, Andrea/Benedetto does the same. He stops at an inn in Compiègne. The next morning, he oversleeps, and upon awakening, finds police lurking around the inn. Benedetto tries escaping through the chimney, but when he finds himself on the roof, decides he must go through yet another one. He sees a chimney that doesn't seem to have a fire going, and goes down it. Coincidentally, that chimney leads to the room inhabited by Eugénie and Louise. They call for help, and Benedetto is arrested.

Chapter 100: The Law

Madame Danglars approaches Villefort. She does not want her family embarrassed, so she asks him to disregard the case against Andrea, which he refuses to do. As they are wrapping up their meeting, they learn that Andrea has been arrested.

Chapter 101: The Apparition

For four days, Valentine has suffered from the effects of the brucine. On the fourth night, a mysterious figure sneaks to her bedside. It is the Count. He tells her that he has been keeping an eye on her from the house next door, exchanging the poison that someone has been putting into her glass each night with an effective antidote. He advises her to not reveal his plan, but instead, to pretend to be sleeping as per the murderer's plan and then try to identify who has been poisoning her.

Chapter 102: The Serpent

Valentine obeys the Count's plan. While pretending to be sleeping, she witnesses Madame d'Villefort pouring poison into her glass. When the Count returns, Valentine asks him why her own stepmother would try to kill her. The Count explains that she wants Valentine's inheritance for her son, Edward. Valentine's first reaction is to feel sorry for Edward for having such an evil mother. Since she cannot actually expose Madame d'Villefort herself, the Count contrives another scheme: as he gives her another pill to take, he tells Valentine that she must trust him unconditionally. She follows his advice and takes the pill.

Analysis: Chapters 94 through 102

The Count is truly moved by the extent of Maximilian's love for Valentine. It puts a change in him in motion. It also allows him to see the genuinely kind and decent Valentine in a light other than as the daughter of Villefort, his enemy, and therefore deserving of his contempt. This is the first sign that the Count is not invulnerable. He realizes that cannot continue painting people with broad strokes, making generalizations about their character based on their lineage.

Danglars and Andrea, both immoral at the core, are cut from the same cloth. They share undesirable traits such as greed and avarice, and will stomp on anyone or anything that presents an obstacle to their ambition. Danglars has no remorse over securing a miserable fate for Eugénie, just as long as he gets his hands on Andrea's wealth. Andrea/Benedetto, correspondingly, has no remorse for killing his foster mother, the woman who helped save his life, and is willing to do the same to the Count, even though he suspects he is his father and it would open the door to an inheritance. One man is more deceitful and unethical than the other –

it is no wonder that their respective demises are intertwined.

Unlike Danglars and Benedetto, Valentine is pure innocence, and is thusly a great contrast to the evil around her. Her inability to, for example, understand why her stepmother would want her dead is a throwback to when Dantès was rendered confused by his unjust imprisonment. Just as she cannot fathom someone acting with such hatred, he could not fathom his friends turning on him. But that is where the comparison ends. Dantès morphed into a vengeance machine, whereas Valentine's innocence is a constant.

Eugénie is an interesting figure with similarities to Valentine as well. Both women want to live their lives independently, love whom they want to love, and pursue their dreams. As the more passive of the two, Valentine cannot bring herself to be disobedient or disrespectful; however, Eugénie is fully capable of rebelling against the norm and what is expected of her, even if it means alienating her family. Valentine hopes for better things; Eugénie makes better things happen herself. Her unorthodox way of life is reminiscent of the Count's own posture of living life according to his own rules and not those of society.

Chapters 103-108

Chapter 103: Valentine

The next day, it appears that Valentine has died. Madame d'Villefort enters her room and finds her lifeless body. She immediately throws out the remaining contents in the glass by her bedside, then cleans it out; however, when she returns to the room later with the rest of the family who now knows about Valentine's death, the sees that the glass has been refilled. The doctor who has been summoned recognizes the contents as poison, and Madame d'Villefort faints.

Chapter 104: Maximilian

A grief-stricken Maximilian enters Valentine's room, disturbing her father, Villefort, who is by her bed. Because Villefort doesn't know who he is, he banishes him from the house. Maximilian leaves, but after a while returns, this time with Noirtier. He confesses his undying love for Valentine, and in a moment of shared misery, Villefort takes pity on him. Maximilian proclaims that revenge must be sought for her death. Noirtier implies that he knows who killed his beloved granddaughter, and asks for a moment alone with his son. Once the others are allowed back into the room, Noirtier and Villefort ask that for now, they keep the murder under wraps. Abbé Busoni, the Villeforts's neighbor, is summoned to pray over the body. Once he is alone with Noirtier, the "priest" explains the plan that has been set into motion.

Chapter 105: Danglars's Signature

When the Count goes to visit Danglars, he finds him writing five checks for one million francs each as payment to the hospital. The Count asks for the checks, as he has a line of credit with Danglars. In a bind, Danglars agrees, a he doesn't want to reveal his dire financial straits. As the Count leaves, the Commissioner of Hospitals arrives for payment. He cannot believe that Danglars just gave away the five million francs intended for him. Danglars promises that the sum will be returned the next day, at which time he will pay the Commissioner. His real plan, however, is to leave during the night to escape his creditors once and for all, as he will never be able to recover financially and pay them back.

Chapter 106: The Cemetery of Père-la-Chaise

As Valentine's funeral takes place, the Count keeps an eye on Maximilian, who is overcome with sorrow. Afterwards, he goes with Maximilian to Julie and Emmanuel's house. Maximilian tells his sister and brother-in-law that he is going to take his own life. To dissuade him, the Count tells Maximilian who he really is, and the role is has played in the Morrel family's life. Maximilian is touched and moved, and wants to share the secret with Julie. The Count asks him to keep their secret. He also promises to reveal who he is to Julie and Emmanuel on one condition: that Maximilian stay with him for a month and not kill himself. If after a month he is still in utter despair, the Count tells Maximilian that he will help him with the suicide.

Chapter 107: The Division

Danglars leaves in despair, fleeing his creditors. Filled with anxiety, Madame Danglars seeks consolation from Lucien Debray. She goes to his hotel room to share with him the letter her husband left, explaining his actions. The letter states that Danglars is bankrupt due to an unexplainable stretch of unusual financial mishaps, and that he cannot meet the obligations to the hospital. Madame Danglars hopes for some kind of comfort from Debray (after all, are were lovers), but he disappoints her by taking a "strictly business" approach to the problem. He gives her half of the money they earned through their illegal insider trading activities, for which they used Danglars's money; however, it is obvious that Debray is no longer interested in Madame Danglars in any personal way, as her main attraction – her access to unlimited funds – has been eliminated. He makes his new attitude known to her.

While Madame Danglars is with Debray, Albert and Mercédès are in another room in the same hotel, discussing their next steps. Albert has enlisted in the army, and by doing so was given a small stipend. He gives his mother the money to pay for her journey to Marseilles, where she will, hopefully, find the money the Count promised. As they depart, they see Debray and Madame Danglars. Debray is impressed by the contrast between the two women, their priorities, and their respective reactions to life's challenges. Madame Danglars is still motivated by greed, whereas Mercédès seeks a better, more honorable life for herself and her son.

The next day, the Count watches as Albert bids his mother farewell. He settles her into a coach headed for Marseilles. The Count makes a promise to himself that he will ensure their happiness no matter what it takes.

Chapter 108: The Lions' Den

Bertuccio visits Benedetto in prison. Still believing that the Count is his biological father, Benedetto is waiting for him to get him out of jail. Bertuccio continues to be annoyed by Benedetto's attitude. He tells him that he is there to explain who his father actually is, but before he can, the men are interrupted. He tells Benedetto that he will come back the next day to reveal the entire story.

Analysis: Chapters 103 through 108

Villefort and Danglars continue on their downward spirals as their worst traits bring about their ruin. Danglars loses his money and his daughter because of his greed, while Villefort's ambition destroys him and his family, even to the point of compromising his daughter's life. And in spite of all the ruination that surrounds them, neither man seeks redemption or voices a shred of contrition.

As previously noted, Eugénie and Valentine, while similar, also possess decided contrasts in personality. The same could be said for Madame Danglars and Mercédès. Both women have suffered at the hands of their husbands, although Mercédès's suffering is of a less superficial nature. However, as Debray notices, there is nothing similar in the way that the two react to their misfortunes. It can be argued that Madame Danglars is not that much better than her husband – she is deceitful and disloyal, and still believes that she has been dealt an unfair hand. Mercédès, who has lived a decent life and had no part in her husband's crimes, does not play the victim card, but instead, seeks a way to recapture her honor which has been tainted by association. Instead of being taken over by resentment (as has Madame Danglers), she is grateful for the opportunity for a life renewed.

The contrast between the women further underscores an important theme in the novel, that being, how one's outlook can, and does, influence one's contentment. From a purely dispassionate standpoint, Madame Danglars's situation is less grave: she still has a considerable amount of wealth, and the loss of her husband does not cause anything even close to heartbreak, as she holds no true affection for him. Still, much like Caderousse, she cannot stop complaining about her current lot and feels she has not done anything to deserve it. Mercédès, by contrast, is now poor and alone (save for her son), but still manages to accept the reality of circumstances and try to make the best of it. With the same strength and perseverance displayed by Julie and Emmanuel, she forges ahead with dignity in the hopes that something better will be on the other side of the journey.

Chapters 109-113

Chapter 109: The Judge

Villefort begins building the case against Benedetto. When the trial comes to pass, he tells his wife that although he has known that she is a murderer, to save his own social standing, he will not shed light on her crimes and bring about her death by execution. Instead, Villefort tells his wife to kill herself, using the same poison she has been using to kill others, among them, his first wife's parents. If she has not done so by the time he returns from court, he promises her that he will expose her crimes and order the authorities to execute her at once.

Chapter 110: The Assizes

Benedetto's trial becomes a main social attraction, and all of Paris wants to be a part of it. Aristocrats clamor to get into the courthouse to see it. Once on the stand, Benedetto makes the surprise announcement that he is Villefort's son – the one his father conceived out of wedlock and buried alive until saved by Bertuccio. The court asks for proof, but Villefort admits to it all.

Chapter 111: Expiation

Villefort heads home after his horrific day in court. Realizing that he has no right to judge the actions of his wife considering his own crimes, he decides that he will let her live, and that the two of them will leave Paris and start a new life somewhere outside of France. But when he arrives, he sees that he is too late, as she has already killed herself and her son, Edward. Seeking comfort for his grief, Villefort goes to his father, Noirtier, who is visiting Abbé Busoni. The Abbé tells Villefort that he is actually Edmond Dantès. Villefort drags Dantès to the dead bodies of his wife and son, asking Dantès if his acts of revenge are finished. Seeing the dead boy affects Dantès, who reacts with sorrow. He tries to revive him with the elixir he used previously, but fails. Dantès then tells Villefort that Valentine is not really dead, hoping that will ease his grief, but by this point, Villefort has lost his mind. The sight of all this turmoil and tragedy makes Dantès rethink his acts of self-designed justice. When he returns home, he tells Maximilian that they are departing Paris the next morning.

Chapter 112: The Departure

The next day, Maximilian bids farewell to Julie and Emmanuel, then leaves Paris with the Count. As they depart, the Count states that his mission to avenge the wrongdoings of his enemies is now complete.

Chapter 113: The House in the Allées de Meillan

The Count and Maximilian arrive in Marseilles. They watch as Albert leaves for Africa on his first military assignment. Maximilian then visits the gravesite of his father, while the Count goes to see Mercédès in the former home of Louis Dantès. He tells her that he will always help Albert in any way possible. Mercédès shares her feelings that her current situation must be her fate; the Count replies that man also has free will.

The Count then goes to meet Maximilian at Morrel's grave, and tells him to remain in Marseilles while he goes to Italy for a few days.

Analysis: Chapters 109 through 113

Edward's death underlines the conflict within the Count that started earlier in the book that being, questioning whether or not his mission is a sound, justifiable and noble one. Now that his actions have brought about the death of an innocent, he cannot help but ask if his path was misguided. This shock to his system compromises the Count's conviction that he is something of a divine instrument of justice.

There are some recovered versions of the novel which include what could very well have been a pivotal scene: after all is said and done, the Count returns to Château d'If in search of a sign from God to tell him his actions were justified. He finds an old manuscript of Faria's which opens with a biblical quote: "Thou shalt tear out the teeth of the dragon and trample the lion's underfoot, thus saith the Lord." In current versions which do not include this moment, there is never any validation that his actions were aligned with God's will, therefore leaving the Count is a state of doubt.

This process of chipping away at the Count's seeming infallibility is also illustrated through the failure of his elixir to save Edward. His potions have always worked in the past, just as he has always been victorious in his actions against his enemies since escaping Château d'If. Now that the elixir has failed, so must the Count acknowledge his own limitations. Although heroic on some levels, he is not a god; he cannot revive the dead, and his mission comes into doubt.

The Count's final encounter with Mercédès raises the question of free will, or proactivity, versus God's will, or passivity. Mercédès believes that her life has unfolded according to a divine plan, whereas the Count takes a posture that is diametrically opposed. For him, the ability to choose is what makes life worth living. All that matters is the individual's ability to remain an individual, and by doing so, a person fulfills God's true plan. Sadly, it can be argued that Mercédès's inability to assert her own will is what brought about her current situation, as had she been stronger, she would not have married Fernand in the first place. She sealed her fate on that day.

Dumas's treatment of his women characters can be perceived as biased against women in general. The two women who have the biggest hearts yet suffer the most are Valentine and Mercédès. They are also held up as pillars of femininity, entwining this trait with what is, in the author's mind, acceptable and appealing in women. The action is primarily seen among the male characters, with the exception of Eugénie, who is not considered womanly but instead, masculine in nature. She is the only female character to decide her own fate, but by doing so, excludes herself from being considered feminine. Going on this premise, it is apparent that true femininity is defined and accompanied by passivity, and since passivity is superseded, or "trumped," by individualism, the female gender is somehow delegated to a back seat to men.

Suicide is a widely incorporated motif in Romantic literature, as it acts as an immediate solution to the feeling of painful solitude, loneliness or heartache. For example, Maximilian vows to end his life if Valentine marries Franz d'Epinay. Haydée states the same in response to the possibility of the Count leaving her. Depending on one's viewpoint, there is innate irony here, as suicide can be interpreted as the ultimate act of passivity – a final resignation, a "giving up." It goes completely against the grain of the Count's mantra of being proactive and controlling your own destiny. Or, does it? To some, suicide is the ultimate act of independence. To call when and how you will die, and to execute the means yourself, is the apex of control.

Chapters 114-117

Chapter 114: Peppino

Danglars has gone to Italy where he presents the Count's receipt for five million francs to the investment firm of Thomas and French. He intends to resettle in Vienna with the money, once against letting greed overcome him. Peppino, who is now a member of Luigi Vampa's bandit party, has learned about this scheme, so he follows Danglars to the firm.

The following day, Danglars is ambushed and captured by the bandits while he is travelling from Rome to Venice. They bring Danglars to Vampa, who puts him in a jail cell. Danglars's only comfort is that he believes that had the bandits wanted him dead, they would have killed him by now. He suspects he has been kidnapped for ransom. He goes to sleep on the cot in his cell, thinking that with a bit of patience on his part, he will be freed.

Chapter 115: Luigi Vampa's Bill of Fare

The next morning, Danglars is starving. He asks for food, and is told that he can have anything he wants for the inflated cost of one hundred thousand francs. Too hungry to argue, he buys a very expensive chicken.

Chapter 116: The Pardon

The next day, Vampa tells Danglars that he is acting on someone else's orders by holding him. He also states that the food costs are out of his hands as well.

Almost two weeks pass, and Danglars is almost broke from buying ridiculously priced food. He has only fifty thousand francs left, so he makes to decision to hold onto it and eat nothing else no matter how hungry he gets. But his hunger overwhelms him, and he begs for food. In response, he hears a voice that asks him if he is sorry for his past wrongdoings. Danglars says that yes, he is, and wants to repent for them. The Count reveals himself as the man behind the voice, and goes on to tell Danglars that he is actually Edmond. Because Danglars sought forgiveness and redemption, he is freed and left on the side of a back road. Monte Cristo steps into the light and tells Danglars that he is forgiven. He approaches a brook for water, and notices that his hair has turned completely white.

Chapter 117: The Fifth of October

Maximilian's month-long arrangement with the Count is coming to a close. On that very day, he heads for the island of Monte Cristo to meet the Count, and expresses that without Valentine, he still wants to die. The Count brings him to a beautiful palace which has been built into the coastal rocks. He then tries to discern whether or not the young man's love for Valentine is unwavering by tempting him with every conceivable pleasure and even the entirety of his fortune. Maximilian rejects them all, wanting only to die from loneliness without his love. The Count acts as if he is acquiescing, and gives Maximilian a potion. The young man believes it to be poison and drinks it immediately, falling into a heavy sleep. Valentine enters. The Count tells her that she must always be faithful to Maximilian, as his love for her is pure and unselfish. As an act of gratitude for bringing them together, he requests that Valentine ensure Haydée's well-being now that he will be leaving her. Haydée enters as he says this, and asks for an explanation. The Count tells her that he is going to return her to her proper station as princess, and that she must give up the notion of a life with him. He is going to begin a personal journey of self-reflection to seek God's forgiveness and repent for his sins. Haydée responds by saying that she would sooner kill herself than not be with him. The two envelope one another, and for the first time in all these years, the Count has a sense that real love and happiness can be his. He tells her that his intention was to relinquish their relationship as a form of penance, but now believes that God, by sending him Haydée's love, has forgiven his actions and intends for them to remain together. Maximilian awakens to see Valentine waiting for him.

The next morning, Maximilian and Valentine realize that the Count and Haydée have left the island. They find a letter from him that tells them to sail to Leghorn, where they will find Noirter waiting for them. The old man will help orchestrate their wedding. The Count also writes that he has left all of his land in France as well as his assets on the island to them in honor of their marriage. Finally, the letter conveys the Count's lesson in the arrangement he made with Maximilian: he wanted the young man to realize beyond a shadow of a doubt that life is always more desirable than death, and the only way to really learn that is to recover from despair. One can only be capable of experiencing true bliss if he or she has experienced true despair. He closes with the statement, "All human knowledge is contained in these two words: Wait and Hope."

Analysis: Chapters 114 through 117

This last section wraps up the very long, complicated, sometimes arduous journey of the Count of Monte Cristo. It also drives home the point of the Count's realization that he is not godlike in his talents or abilities, but has limits just like the rest of the human race. By the time the Count is ready to deal with Danglars, it appears that his own actions reflect this sentiment, as he intervenes just before Danglars risks starving to death. The Count of a few chapters earlier may have thought that he had some kind of divinely ordained power to save the man; but this Count now knows that he must not take away a man's life, or mental stability, or family. Not every action can be rationalized as an act of justice regardless of ramifications. So even though Danglars is destitute, he still has his life and is in possession of his sanity, which is more than what can be said for Fernand and Villefort. One can still have a valid, authentic life without also having the trappings of wealth. And, by allowing Danglers his freedom – and more important, his life – the Count keeps the door open for true, compete repentance and redemption. Death would prevent these from ever even being a possibility. Still, his punishment is nonetheless appropriate, as he loses the one thing he holds dear – money.

Dumas structures the story so that each enemy's punishment from the Count is tailor-made, hitting him where it hurts the most and closely reflecting the character of his specific crime. Even the way the Count drives each man's demise is related to the same. Danglars, whose greed and jealousy over the young sailor's appointment as captain of the Pharaon propel him to betray Dantès, lives a subsequent life motivated solely by his desire for money and more money. Ultimately, he is saved, but left penniless. Villefort acted on unbridled ambition, leading to Dantès' unfair imprisonment. Fernand lusts after the woman Dantès loves, but his actions lead to his family deserting him. He has no option but to end his sorry life.

The transformation Dantès experiences after he escapes prison, arrives on the island of Monet Cristo and gains the treasure promised to him by Faria has left him, in many ways, inhuman. Although he has prowess in a multitude of areas, making him seem like something akin to a superhero, his capacity to experience life – really, to feel it - as a full human being is compromised. He knows little of joy, of love or of kindness. It is only after Haydée's love breaks through the hard exterior that he can once again act and react as part the human race. As the saying goes, "Love Conquers All," and this seems to hold true for the Count in particular.

Receiving her love, and experiencing his love for her, he reconnects with those emotions which humanize us. Also, he realizes his own advice to Maximilian: that only by experiencing anguish and despair can one truly appreciate and experience happiness.

The last words of the novel point to the Count's newly found awareness of man's limitations. Although he is consistent and unwavering in his belief that man controls his own destiny, it is not until the end of the novel that he acknowledges that no matter how powerful a man is, or determined, or even driven towards what he considers a greater good, he can never compete with Divine Providence. That, he concedes, is ultimately in the hands of God.

Themes

Revenge

The Count of Monte Cristo is literally filled with the theme of revenge and how it manifests in the actions of the title character, a.k.a. Edmond Dantès. His torturous time in prison ate away at his ability to experience compassion and empathy, and he is consumed with getting back at those responsible and bringing them to what he perceives as justice. Further, it acts as a catalyst to drive the storyline itself, and keeps the reader thoroughly captivated. Once Edmond transforms into the Count of Monte Cristo, revenge is never off the radar, and is almost another character. From a superficial standpoint, it is engaging to watch the Count's plan take shape; however, by the novel's end, the reader has taken the journey with the Count and inevitably comes to the same conclusion as he does: in the final analysis, is revenge a worthwhile pursuit? It is a simple question with an extremely complex answer.

Justice

Edmond Dantès, or rather, the Count, believes he must implement justice on his own terms, as the judicial system is, in his opinion, a failure. Guilty people go free, innocent people are imprisoned, and the best tool for success is a lack of ethics.

Dantès believes that he is acting with God's approval, as he aims to punish the guilty for their crimes and the pain they have caused to others. But the lines blur, as his notion of justice, because it is primarily based in self-satisfaction, crosses over to revenge, and revenge lacks the noble character that true justice carries. Because his notion of justice is somewhat misguided, he must eventually admit that perhaps not all of his actions can be justified, as in the process of implementing them, innocent people have been harmed. This is not the purview of man, but of God. Humans are inferior beings to the divine, and Dantès cannot help but come to that conclusion.

Happiness

Dumas repeatedly visits the theme of happiness, and how one's own attitude can make or break one's level of bliss. He even positions his characters into separate camps: the more appealing, sympathetic and admirable characters are those who can accept their "life circumstances" and see the potential for happiness regardless. The characters who are never satisfied – they never have enough money, or power, or both – are consistently the least happy and the basest of people. In many ways, it is Dumas's version of seeing a glass half empty or half full, only with much more severe ramifications.

Dantès' enemies turn on him partially because of their own discontentment with their own lives. They are jealous of Dantès' success in work and love, and go on the attack as a result. In contrast, Dumas gives the reader Julie and Emmanuel Herbaut, who are filed with love and contentment because they have appropriate priorities. They value those things that truly deserve to be: health, love, tranquility, family.

Loneliness and Alienation

As Dantès rots in prison, he feels himself detaching from the human experience. Progressively alienated and starving for human contact, he begins to lose his own humanity. This loss escalates further after he escapes and starts out on his mission of revenge, as he is still in the clutches of utter hatred and resentment.

It is important to note that Dantès' saving grace in prison is his relationship with Abbé Faria. The old priest acts as his surrogate father, teacher and mentor, and he exposes him to a comprehensive education in the humanities, languages, literature and sciences. This surely saves Dantès from a total breakdown. His affection for Faria keeps a vestige of humanity alive in him. When the priest dies, however, so does that vestige. Dantès becomes an automaton – no emotional life, no ability to feel or love. There is nothing left to keep him connected to the human race. It is not until he realizes that he loves Haydée that he is able to once again enjoy life. In a way, Faria and Haydée are his lifelines. They keep him from sinking so deeply into his own misery that a return is impossible.

Patience

At the end of the novel, Dantès tells Valentine and Maximilian that life can really be summarized in two words: Wait and Hope. His entire life thus far has exemplified that theory, as Dantès spends much of his life waiting: waiting for freedom from prison, waiting for revenge against his enemies, and waiting for justice for the wrong done to him.

On the more positive side, one can argue that Dantès' patience eventually leads him to better things. It took many years, but when he acknowledges his feelings for Haydée, he has arrived at a place of happiness.

Motifs

Monikers and Aliases

There are so many names changes in *The Count of Monte Cristo* that at times, it is hard to keep up. Of course, the obvious names changes have to do with Dantès' various alter egos, personas and disguises. Keeping up with many of the Judeo-Christian imagery that exists in the book, Dantès parallels the divine as depicted in the Old Testament by changing his name according to the need of the situation. For example, as Abbé Busoni, a priest, he is able to extract information under the guise of priestly confidence. People will confess to the Abbé, thinking that there secrets and sins will never be divulged. In turn, the Abbé implements spiritual justice in the name of God. Lord Wilmore, an innocuous-sounding name at that, is used as he performs random acts of kindness and generosity. The persona behind the name is that of an English nobleman, removing himself from Parisian society even further. Sinbad the Sailor also carries a generous persona, but as the name suggests, is somewhat more mysterious, exotic and rogue-like. Finally, his primary alias, the Count of Monte Cristo, references not only his wealth and position, but God himself (Monte Cristo translates into "mountain of Christ"). The Count, at least from where Dantès sits, has an element of the savior to him, avenging wrongdoings and evil acts with the determination of a divine presence.

The name game affects the other characters as well. As their lives evolve, progress and take shape, so do their names reflect these changes, whether they be changes in social status or family loyalty. In the case of the latter, Villefort is a prime example: in order to distance himself from his Bonapartist father, he changes his name from Noirtier, wanting no association with the family moniker for fear that it might thwart his boundless ambitions. Villefort's decision sheds light on his shallow, ruthless character as well: he will stop at nothing, not even compromising his family, to get what he wants. Fernand Mondego, later known as the Count de Morcerf, undergoes a rise in social standing, allowing him to falsely recreate himself as an aristocrat. This underlines his constitutional dishonesty.

Suicide

The idea of suicide pops up repeatedly in *The Count of Monte Cristo*, as at one point or another, many of the characters - Dantès, Monsieur Morrel, Maximilian Morrel, Haydée, Fernand Mondego, Madame d'Villefort, and Albert de Morcerf – consider taking, or do take, this drastic step. Suicide, as depicted by Dumas, corresponds to the concept widely held by the Romantic writers of the time, being that it is a suitable response to unbearable events, particularly a derailed love affair. To some extent, it is even viewed as a barometer for true love. Example: the Count tests Maximilian's love for Valentine by making him postpone his suicide for a month. When the young man is still in despair after 30 days, the Count is convinced that his love is the real thing. Haydée, too, threatens it should the Count leave her.

The characters are not casual or disrespectful when it comes to suicide. On the contrary, they perhaps feel things too strongly and too intensely to not react to the mishaps of life on such a grand scale. Within the microcosm of operatic, high drama that Dumas has created, such behavior is not unusual.

Politics

The Count of Monte Cristo is an adventure novel, but is also an historical one. As such, is charged with political themes and influences taken "from the headlines" of the day. The landscape is peppered with Bonapartists, royalists, rebels, and overly ambitious politicians. Moreover, Dumas makes little secret of with whom his allegiance lies. Most of the characters who are aligned with the tenets of Napoleon are by association considered more sympathetic, e.g. Morrel, Noirtier, and even Dantès, who, as the Count, personifies this ideal to its fullest potential. Conversely, the royalists, or those who are more wrapped up in strict social castes, e.g. Morcerf and Villefort, are in fact depicted as treacherous, conniving and dishonest. They are also prejudiced and greedy, wanting to keep the structure of "haves" versus the "have nots." In the case of Danglars, Dantès' third sworn enemy, is most interested in acquiring money at any cost, regardless of political affiliation. For him, capitalism is king. The author incorporates these affiliations in order to further illustrate and add another layer to each character's core.

Symbolism

Water

Water has long been a literary symbol of cleansing, rebirth and renewal. In *The Count of Monte Cristo*, water is introduced as part of the environment from nearly the first paragraph. Edmond Dantès has chosen the sea as his career, and has excelled at it. It represents his second home, and even though the sea can be threatening, its overall serenity corresponds to his kind and gentle manner. When he has transformed himself into the Count, the sea plays an equally important role. It is the one real constant in his life, and the one place he feels most content, regardless of location. He is always connected to the sea, and always will be.

When Dantès attains his freedom after his long, unjust incarceration, the sea is once again his savior and mistress. It is through water that he escapes, and is cleansed of the horrific experience of Chateau d'If. Once he reaches Monte Cristo, his life changes forever. The metaphor that Dumas incorporates – that of a baptism and rebirth – is not a particularly subtle one but is certainly understandable given the circumstances. It also harkens back to the Christian motifs that are found throughout the book. Still, it is a double-edged sword, as the rebirth that Dantès experiences isn't necessarily a positive one. He does indeed change upon arriving on the island, but the question remains: is the change for the better?

Beyond the cleansing powers of water, it also is life sustaining. Without water there is no life. Water was the instrument through which Dantès gets his life back, and water keeps him steadied and balanced.

Potions and Elixirs

Potions were of great interest to Romantic period writers as well as readers. Clearly, potions have been a staple in love stories for even longer: *Tristan and Iseult*, dating back to the 12th century, for example, as well as Shakespeare's *Romeo and Juliet*. But for Dumas's purposes, the use of an elixir takes center stage in various parts of *The Count of Monte Cristo*. Although elixirs are generally thought to be medicinal and life-saving, the potions used by the Count have the unusual duality of being both fatal and antidotal. This seems to be in line with the Count's grandiose opinion of his own capabilities and influence – in short, his power. Since he believes that he is on a mission of divine intervention, he comes to think of himself as divine as well. This goes on for quite a while in the novel until he is faced with the reality of Edward's untimely and unnecessary death. Initially, he assumes that he can save the boy; however, when his elixir fails miserably, he must confront his delusions that he is godlike. Only God has the power to resurrect the dead; the Count, or Dantès, is, merely mortal.